THE PRICE OF HAPPINESS

THE PRICE OF HAPPINESS

A Novel

David Orsini

THE PRICE OF HAPPINESS

Other Books by David Orsini

Prisoners of Desire

The Enchantments

The Reappearing

The Weaver of Plots

Schemes, Disguises, & Traps

Vanishing by Degrees

The Ghost Lovers

The Woman Who Loved Too Well

The Subtleties of Seduction

Bitterness / Seven Stories

CONTENTS

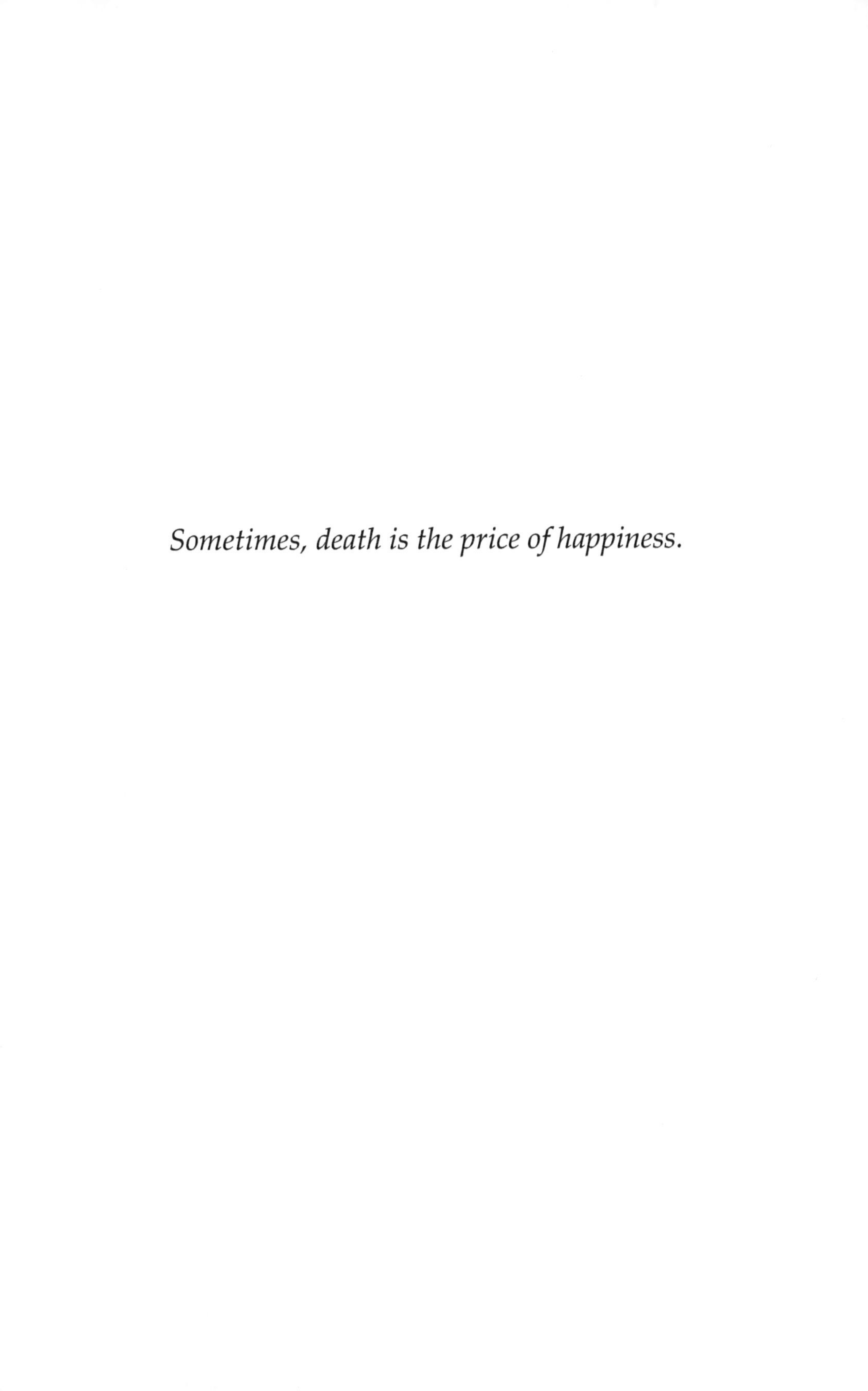

Sometimes, death is the price of happiness.

CHAPTER ONE

A NEW WAY TO SEE

"My granddaughter represents, of course, a special case," Gerald Marnham said. "But I have no reservations about leaving her in your care."

It was not difficult to offer the Aubrays his unqualified approval. After spending a week with them here in his home in Newport, Rhode Island, he was certain that they would be of immense assistance to his granddaughter. But when their visit ended on Monday morning, he had not yet invited them to join the well-qualified staff who maintained the smooth workings of his household. Never precipitate in his judgments, he resumed his business schedule and waited for three days before inviting the Aubrays to return. During this period, they permitted themselves a brief vacation in nearby Nantucket. There, they had been swimming and sailing with friends from Alan's Harvard days.

They were conferring now within the burnished amenities of Gerald's study, sequestered as it was inside the southwest wing of the ample house. Every Thursday he permitted himself to be away from his New York office for a few hours. It had been his custom to arrive in Newport promptly at nine o'clock, after Sommers, his driver for three decades and more, and Robert Finley met him at the train station. He had never admitted to anyone except himself that in their different ways both Sommers and Finley were of immense value to him. His keen-sighted Amanda had known without his ever speaking of the matter. She had known much about him of which she had had the good sense not to speak. Because she had been a more-than-ordinary wife, she understood when it was not necessary to remark upon his habits or his ambition or his business travel across the globe. Nor had she ever questioned his expectation that those in his service must be as punctual and efficient as they were capable.

Death had taken her away from him after they had enjoyed what in retrospect he now told himself had been a marriage of modulated compatibility for thirty-eight years. During these four years without her, he had chosen to remain both ambitious and productive. Rarely did he find time for his Newport home. Most of the time, he was living in New York or in Pittsburgh, London, Paris, and the Orient. But he did not care to sell it, so much did he value the memory of the years he had spent there with Amanda and with their son Austin, who was thriving as a junior executive in the Marnham Steel Corporation, and with their daughter Rebecca and her husband, Kevin Farrell, who had recently died together in a plane crash en route to Pittsburgh.

For this reason most of all, his desire to keep alive his recollection of those happier days, he had regarded Robert Finley as absolutely essential to the efficient management of his Newport estate, with its Federal-period stateliness, ocean-front setting, and twenty-five acres. Trained as a civil engineer, Finley had not merely monitored the upkeep of the property. He had redefined both the natural and the man-made beauty of the land which carried forward the Marnhams' prestige as well as their history. But he, too, had died.

"He just wore out," Evelyn had explained, though no explanations were necessary. An autopsy had revealed a subtle heart malady which had eluded detection even from an eminent cardiologist. But he had appreciated Evelyn Finley's remark, nonetheless. She was a matter-of-fact woman who had loved her husband very much and who would not embarrass his memory with a show of maudlin pieties.

He knew that Finley's death could not be avoided or postponed. Nor had he imagined that anyone coming to the position that Finley had held for twenty-nine years would be as effective—at least, not in the first year. But this week had convinced him that Alan Aubray would—-within the mere span of a year—gradually equal and then exceed

Finley's successes. That Alan would accept only a year's appointment to the post dismayed him, at first. But his decision to move forward to other challenging assignments, once he completed his work of restoration and enhancement, was not surprising. There were many other formidable commissions which even now were beckoning him, not only as a civil engineer and landscape architect, but also as a mechanical and aeronautical engineer.

Strong-bodied and handsome, Alan wore his knowledge and his assurance with a nice understatement. If he was aware that his six-foot stature and his rugged physicality gave him an advantage over those men who were not similarly favored by nature, his quiet authority gave no evidence of narcissistic self-reflection or of a careless displacement of the less impressive persons about him.

There was within his appearance something extraordinary and altogether promising. The well-honed muscularity and the even-tempered manner were, if the truth be told, auspicious elements of his personhood, as were his ruddy complexion, dark hair, brown eyes, and full, sensual lips. His beige linen suit, azure shirt, and royal blue tie with beige and azure swirls enhanced his confident appearance. But his knowledge as a multi-faceted engineer and as a landscape architect, his brave service as a first lieutenant in the recent war, and his realistic view of the world were the elements which gave him a distinctive gravity.

In the years before the war, he completed his undergraduate and graduate studies in civil, mechanical, and aeronautical engineering at the École Polytechnique in Paris. He also spent a year completing a second master's degree in landscape architecture and urban planning at the Harvard Graduate School of Design. Returning to France, he assisted major companies in the designs of roads, canals, and an apartment building, as well as in the planning of pipelines, water distribution systems, and drainage facilities which included bridges, dams, and levees. When the war came a year later, he fought in the French Sixth Army within the center of many savage battles, including the Second Battle of the Marne. There, at Dormans in the summer of 1918, he survived a grievous wound to his chest and wounds just as grievous to his left arm and leg.

Once the war ended, he married Charlotte Dussollier, whom he had met when she was a student at the Sorbonne. By then, after the war when he married her, he was twenty-seven years old. Two years younger than he, Charlotte was a light-skinned beauty with a full-bodied figure. She had titian hair, green eyes, a turned-up nose, and lips that must have brought him a special pleasure when she smiled. At this meeting, she wore with feminine poise a light blue silk chiffon dress. Her genuine interest in the well-being of others made her, Gerald believed, as warm-hearted as she was quick-witted.

She, too, had served in the war. Determined to be of use during that hard time, she enrolled in an accelerated nursing program sponsored by the French Red Cross and by the French Army. Skillful and empathetic, she worked long hours attending the wounded whose bodies the war had left intact and the maimed whose bodies had been deprived of one or more limbs. She also took care of those soldiers who were dying. In the first days when she was assigned to their ward, her nurse's composure nearly failed her. All of these men were young, and their torn bodies and bruised minds still craved life.

The Aubrays had come to New York in May 1920, eighteen months after the war ended. Alan had spent many of those months convalescing in a Paris hospital. He and Charlotte were grateful that they had survived the war. But no longer did they believe that whatever worthwhile contributions they made to the world would change its speckled nature. Still, they were hoping to do their part. They were, in fact, looking to find a measure of contentment through careers that challenged and excited their aspirations.

"Let's bring something original into our work-lives," Alan told Charlotte on the day that they had embarked for an altogether new experience in the United States. "And let's explore our sensuality in new ways, too."

He was pleased at how readily she agreed.

"That might help us to make sense of things," she said.

Their path was made easier than it might have been because of Alan's Harvard connections and because of his friendship with Philippe Fontaine, the curator of the fashionable Courtney Art Gallery in Manhattan. Within a short time, they settled in Greenwich Village and for the next three years made a modest success. Alan secured engineering commissions in New York City, and Charlotte took a teaching post at a private school for girls in Manhattan.

By chance, while he was attending the exhibit of canvases by Caillebotte, Pissarro, and Matisse at the Courtney, Gerald mentioned to Philippe and to his wife Emmanuelle that he was in search of a teacher and companion for his granddaughter. Mrs. Fontaine had been a loyal friend of Amanda ever since their days at Bryn Mawr. Through the years she and Philippe had shared many festive occasions with the Marnham family. It was only natural that she should inquire how Eleanor, who was still grieving because of the death of her parents, was faring now that she had graduated from her school in Connecticut. Though he did not explain the girl's troubled residence at the school, Gerald did remark that he had decided that his granddaughter would—-for the next year, at least—continue her studies privately, with an excellent teacher as her guide before she began her college days.

"Could you recommend a suitable young woman for the position?" he asked.

He was not surprised that Emmanuelle could recommend such a woman. Mrs. Fontaine knew everyone who mattered in New York, from the Mellons, Rockefellers, and Astors to the designers and builders of the city. She knew, as well, the significant hoteliers and chefs, the most notable jewelers, milliners and couturiers, and highly regarded painters, musicians, and playwrights. She also knew the Aubrays. Before the war, when she and Philippe spent part of their summers on the French Riviera, they traveled in the same circle as Alan's parents. Georges Aubray was a distinguished surgeon who had made a fortune for himself through his wise investments in New York and Paris real estate. When he and Bérénice retired to their home in South America, she and Philippe saw them less often. Then the war came, and-—except for an extended visit to their home in Buenos Aires—-they saw them not at all.

But during the three years just passed, Philippe and Emmanuelle had renewed their friendship here in New York with Alan. They had heard about his brave war service and about his plan to rely upon himself more than upon his father's wealth to make his way in the world. There was no enmity between him and his father. He counted himself among the fortunate, of course, that his father had insisted that, as a wedding gift, he now accept as an early portion of his inheritance a substantial portfolio of stocks and bonds and real estate holdings and an impressive bank account.

By launching himself on a path different from that of his father, he was actually carrying forward an Aubray tradition. Both his grandfather, who had made his mark as a general in the French Army and later as a prime minister of France, and his father had thrived in different careers. Already, Alan had proved himself as a brave soldier. If he were alive, his grandfather would have been very pleased by his conduct in the war. Now Alan was beginning to make a success as a civil engineer. His recent commissions had honed his excellence as an environmental designer and as a landscape architect.

Alan's wife, Charlotte, had also enjoyed a privileged upbringing. Her father was a senior officer in the French Diplomatic Corps. Currently, he represented France in Indochina. Charlotte had recently completed her third year of teaching at the excellent Newbury School in Manhattan. There, she had guided girls from privileged backgrounds not unlike her own through advanced studies in foreign languages, modern history, the sciences, and mathematics.

But, according to Emmanuelle, she had grown dismayed by the school's old-fashioned pedagogy, which she believed constrained her students' academic venturing and their originality. It was her plan now to seek a teaching post independent from the confines of Newbury or of any school that in subtle ways sponsored lock-step conformity. A formalist with a modern perspective who appreciated none the less the wisdom of tradition, she wanted to help a young woman of eighteen to become not merely knowledgeable, but also self-reliant and inventive. Properly educated in this regard, the girl—who was no longer a girl but a bright and inquiring woman—would bring to the wider world a pragmatic realism, a discreet aptitude for self-testing, and decorous joie-de-vivre.

Hearing all these good things about the Aubrays, Gerald began to think about inviting both Alan and Charlotte to join his Newport staff for a year—Charlotte as teacher and confidante to his granddaughter and Alan as the manager of the estate, a worthy replacement for Finley. But he would move cautiously.

"I'll invite them to spend a week in Newport," he told Emmanuelle after she had offered a favorable biography of young Aubrey and his wife. "I'd like to find out whether they relate well to the place and to my granddaughter."

That they related supremely well to the Newport

scene, their success with the other members of his staff, with the friends whom he invited to meet them at a week-end party, and with his granddaughter made very clear. What impressed him most of all, probably because his need of a timely replacement for Finley seemed far more crucial than his acquiring a governess for his granddaughter, was the genuine fervor which Alan brought to his comprehensive survey of the property. No sooner had he mentioned to the young man that he wanted to revise and expand both the landscape and the buildings which defined his Newport estate, than Alan set to work photographing with his Leica every portion of the property. Using these photographs as a frame of reference, he then composed a set of architectural design plans that meant to invoke changes as functional as they were beautiful.

Accompanying him on many of these photo sessions, Gerald became aware that Alan found his proper niche in the direct statement and precise rendering of a scene. He was a gifted landscape architect drawn to photography as an instrument for documenting designed space and exploring the many reciprocal facets of an environment. He studied all of space in terms of its natural forms and human alterations, its urban and rural extensions, and its multiple possibilities for current use or for future transformation.

Insightful as much as it was empirical, his camera-eye keenly apprehended within the twenty-five-acre property the elegant interplay of glacial history, ocean expanse and human habitation. His photographs recorded the full character of the place. Their imagery showed the sumptuous in association with the stark, the vast with the intimate. Now the place must advance the good work that Finley had accomplished. Prudent revisions and additions must link the current with the timeless.

The plans that Alan designed would maintain the Federal-period stateliness of the house and, at the same time, introduce a modernism which carried itself with minimalist sweep and elongated lines.

Discreetly, the Marnham estate would assert that tremendous natural forces had yielded compatibly and handsomely to the presence of human beings. It was this authentic statement which would give to the property an extraordinary solidity fashioned from a shared design at once pragmatic and civil. Already, the main house claimed its own expressive individuality. It was located not at the water's edge, but farther back into the land, gaining thereby elevation and foreground and prospect. Yet a new configuration would neither neglect nor compromise Gerald's desire to be near the ocean. A swimming pool and pool house and pergola, emblematic of the human will activating its own propensities, would fan outward to the water's edge below the main house. These forms would be enhanced by and imbued with the luster of the main house's ocean perch.

Compelling, too (so Alan's plan indicated) would be the indigenous fraternity of seventy-five native oaks. Transplanted from a meadow nearby, they would define in various locations on the property their admirable congruence with the pristine land and with the billowing ocean. Although they had been stunted by salt air and strong winds, several of these trees would find their places in the arrival area of the estate. Each of them would be pruned and replanted to emphasize their mottled bark and natural distortions and to claim this seaward habitation as their proper heritage.

Gerald was equally impressed with Alan's revision of the entry drive as one confronted it from a southerly direction. Idiosyncratic, his plan accentuated topography. It enabled the drive to traverse rolling dips and knolls and to skirt contours before arriving at the main house. Not far from the house he would build a new garage and several guest cottages, each of them stone-clad and hunkered into the earth. According to his plan, one must step down three feet in order to enter them. These buildings would catch and distill the undulating land into a singular plane, which would then descend from the north side toward the ocean. The banked expanse of lawn would address without challenging the restless sea's monumentality.

As a landscape architect and as a civil engineer, Alan translated the truth of his seeing through direct statements about the external environment. His was a precise apprehension of implicated structures and symbiotic relationships.

"It's all about connectedness," Alan explained after Gerald praised his ingenuity. "It's all about the ways that we relate to one another and to the natural and man-made forms which surround us."

"Well, I like your plans very much," Gerald told him on the Monday that the Aubreys were leaving for their brief visit to Nantucket. They would drive there in the reliable comforts of their Bentley.

He was happy to tell Alan so once again on the bright Thursday morning in the week following the Aubrays' first visit. They were conferring in his study, where he had just announced to him and to Charlotte their appointments to his staff. "I think both of you will be very good for this place."

Conferring with him in his study more than a week after she and Alan had first met him, Charlotte found herself ambivalently impressed by Gerald Marnham's command of a scene. He was a tall, stately assurance made austere and gaunt by time's unflinching ordinances. Yet to her eyes he was no less a resilient aptitude and a staid ballast withstanding the world's confusion and indecorousness. How supremely well-ordered he was and perhaps always had been. The coherent accuracies that defined him were reflected not only in the color coordinates of his navy linen suit, royal blue silk shirt, and sky-blue paisley necktie. Those accuracies were also reflected in the very room where they were conversing.

In this specific moment of their meeting, just after he had invited Alan and her to join his staff, he was seated, implacable and straight-backed, at his desk. It was a nineteenth-century bow-fronted mahogany pedestal partnered handsomely with a green leather top. The round brass pulls on its drawers embellished a distinctive aesthetic. During a carefully modulated encounter, she recognized the balance and proportion and intricate clarity of this special room of Gerald's.

While maintaining the requirements of their own discreet equilibrium, she and Alan were seated within the comforts of Carlyle chairs. Their generously padded, button-tufted backs and fixed seat cushions were an Edwardian abundance, as were the serene-rich hues in stripes of beige and gold and navy. Their maple legs on brass casters enhanced a correct and amplified solidity.

Quietly seated on Alan's right, she noticed how effectively the room became a metaphoric continuation of the exterior life unfolding around and upon his property. For there, on the high-ceilinged, pale-yellow wall behind and above the desk where Gerald sat, the vivid splendors of Monet's *Regattas at Argenteuil* complemented and intensified the summer day's grand propensities—all the excited imagery informing the expansive arched windows that opened to a garden and to the sea nearby.

That imagery offered to her glance as she faced Gerald and faced, as well, the windows' sumptuous prospect beyond and to the right of him, colorful sailboats that rose upon her seeing like bright flares in the distance hurrying across cerulean, sun-mottled waters. Mastering its own ascension, inhabiting as it did the wall directly behind and above Gerald's desk in vaulted, cathedral space, the extraordinary *Regattas* with correspondent powers also vitalized the spacious circumference of a discriminating man's study. Surely, on this canvas Monet not only emulated Nature's implicated harmonies. He also taught the spectator visiting it how, more authentically, to see.

Subtly and deftly, Monet teaches us to see. So, in keen attentiveness Charlotte mused as she first entered the room and before she imparted her wish to be for Eleanor Farrell the auspicious influence the young woman needed if she was to be rescued. Braced by new perceiving (she told herself), we accept the aggregate of blotches in the lower part of the picture as gestures of paint translating colored ripples on the water. Broad, italic strokes clarify the painter's act even as they reflect and guide us to the upper part of the canvas and the instantly discernible reality of amber-luminous sailboats, cobalt-green hedges and trees, and houses wearing emphatic red roofs beneath an understated azure sky.

Still the bright flares that were sailboats flourished within sight of Gerald's property and upon her scanning glance toward the arched windows of his study before which she sat. Still their kinetic, sailing rhythms went on hurrying across sun-mottled Newport waters in the cerulean distance.

There was, she felt, something happily artful about this juxtaposition of Monet's canvas on the wall behind and above Gerald's desk and of the Newport seascape quickening the prospect beyond the windows of his study. This melding of literal and metaphoric and of outside world and inner reflected the balance and coherence of the life that Gerald Marnham invited to unfold around him. It was this disciplined symmetry and its scrupulously designed perfection which (she imagined) he sought as the most meaningful pattern of life—his life in particular and the lives of his son and his granddaughter.

Yet, Monet's complicity with Nature located the spontaneous in energetic daring. His peerless seeing was an extemporary gesture or seemed so. There was little of that art in Gerald's engagement with reality. In fact, there was very little of that liberality we call instinct or intuition and, sometimes, adventure. For Monet (and, yes, for Eleanor, too—she had the same spirit) all of life was an astonishing kaleidoscope. It was a veritable stereopticon inviting each of us to define our own arts through its many colors. But Gerald, though an immensely successful corporate leader, did not seek the full spectrum of life. It was not his way to experience the manifold colors of life or to test their vibrancies and hidden values. Instead, he worked from the subdued palette which hesitates to identify its proficiencies through unconstrained gesture or willful experiment or impulsive daring.

So, Charlotte believed. From his casual remarks about his relations with the daughter who had died and with a son who strove to fulfill his father's will, she was aware that Gerald had become inflexible in his prescriptions for their well-being. Even while experiencing a subdued dismay at his paternal arbitrariness, though, she respected him for heeding the voice of his own conscience. Yet that respect and admiration would not keep her from quietly invoking a more realistic program concerning Eleanor's future.

Before she expressed herself once more as the teacherly advocate of Eleanor's happiness, Gerald reinforced his own opinion of his granddaughter's situation. At this time, he moved away from his desk and took his place in the handsome Chelsea wing chair beside her. Its navy vintage linen was trimmed with antiqued brass nail-heads, which represented another clarified proportion upon her senses. Since they had been speaking about Eleanor, he directed his words now to her rather than to Alan, who observed them in tactful silence. While facing her with a courtliness which pleased her womanly self-regard even as it revealed his patrician reserve, Gerald mentioned once again that she was going to be the essential component in his rescuing plan for Eleanor.

"You must bring her back to life again," he said.

After the deaths of her parents, Gerald had explained in their first meeting, his eighteen-year-old granddaughter suffered a breakdown. But, when she read the reports of Eleanor's teachers and of the psychiatrist who had lately counseled her, Charlotte believed that the girl's emotional problems had begun long before her parents had died. Eleanor's fear that they had abandoned her began when she was a little girl of four or five. Then and later, her parents were often away, busy with their careers as corporate executives. Their responsibilities often required them to be not only in Pittsburgh, but also in New York, London, Paris, and Shanghai.

Her mother and her father had, nevertheless, carefully monitored her education in the earliest years when an aged governess was teaching her at home, when a young married couple named Sheffield were also guiding her education, and after that, when she attended Miss Porter's, a private school in Farmington, Connecticut. They wanted their daughter to be as knowledgeable and as poised as she was lovely and successful. They had little empathy for her shy reticence. To win their favor, Eleanor had always excelled in her studies and in other learning activities, which included horse-riding, swimming, and skiing. She had also become a fine painter and a gifted pianist. At school, she had willed herself to be a leader. She became the captain of the tennis and swimming teams and the president of her class.

Although she enjoyed her popularity and the feminine loveliness which she had inherited from her mother, her uneasiness about her relationship with her parents never left her. When they did find time to be with her, they wanted to hear not that she had missed them, but that she had made many new achievements at school. Only then, after she had shown them the favorable reports of her teachers, did they permit themselves to embrace her and to allow her to kiss them.

"But this success is only the beginning," her mother most often and sometimes her father would remind her. "There is a great deal more that you must accomplish if you want to take an important place in the world."

After they were killed while traveling in their private plane to the headquarters of the Marnham Steel

Corporation in Pittsburgh, Eleanor struggled through the hard days of her grief. Through those last months of her senior year, the affection of her peers and the motherly counsel of her teachers did assuage her grief, though without dispelling it. In those last months before her graduation, enhanced as it was by academic honors, she spent some after-school hours conferring with a psychiatrist who specialized in the care of young adults. Because of his wise treatment and her willingness to explore with unstinting honesty the person that she had thus far become, she began to be well again. After many months of receiving wise counsel from her psychiatrist and after her graduation from her private school, she made her new home with her grandfather. That was two weeks ago. Her grandfather's plan for her—endorsed as well by her psychiatrist—required her prudence and patience. She must push back her entrance into Bryn Mawr. A year of home study, a more relaxed schedule of New England travel, and convivial fellowship with her peers would help her retrieve her lost happiness and the young woman named Eleanor Farrell, whose confident identity she believed she had also lost.

Aware of the challenge that he was setting for his granddaughter and for himself, Gerald was counting on Charlotte's proficiencies as Eleanor's teacher and as her confidante.

"Eleanor needs a teacher who can also be a helpful friend," Gerald said. "She needs to believe that even without her parents she can make her way in the world very effectively."

"You want her to become self-reliant," she said. "I, too, believe that is the essential lesson which she must master."

With quiet intonations, she was reinforcing his point of view.

"After spending last week in her company, I am confident that with the proper guidance she will learn how to believe in herself."

"Ah, yes," he said. "*That* is what she has lost."

"I'll teach her how to meet the surprise of the world." Already, she could see, he appreciated her solicitous regard of his granddaughter. So, perceiving, with carefully measured timbres he offered new words to reinforce his approval of her plan for Eleanor.

"The timing could not be better. She's eighteen years old now and must soon make her way in the wider world. Before losing her parents, she had learned to be a confident young lady. She must retrieve what she has lost. She must win back her self-assurance. You can help her to win back her best self. Keep in mind that, after this year of home study, she will be in Pennsylvania at Bryn Mawr College, her grandmother's alma mater. Even with teachers and friends around her, she will have to rely upon her own capacities if she's going to succeed at being an individual."

"She was learning to be very successful as a self-determining individual before she lost her parents. She can learn to be so again."

Once again, he found matter-of-fact words meant to reaffirm the importance of Eleanor's new schedule.

"Her Bryn Mawr plans for next year make her association with you even more important. You are the one person who can help Eleanor to become her best self again. In fact, your positive influence will help her to rally from her grief and at the same time to advance in her studies."

"A year from now she will be strong again and well-prepared," she answered him. The cool poise of her voice defined her conviction. "On her own, Eleanor is going to make you very proud of her."

She rose gracefully from her chair. Alan's glance upon her intimated that her subdued beauty was a proper ascension in that moment dominating the room, until he and Gerald rose to meet her. As Gerald brought to her the manly composure that was his ingrained authority, his formality was as harnessed as he cared to make it. He took her delicate hands, decorous now with white summer gloves, into his own and clasped them in a finely measured expression of his gratitude for her belief in Eleanor's value and in that troubled girl's ability to make a scrupulous grandfather proud.

"I must confess that I am looking forward to such a time," he said. "For then I'll be convinced that she has come to know herself better."

He watched as she turned to join Alan just before the three of them began making their way out of his study.

"You can be a part of this, too," he told Alan. "Eleanor might even come to see both of you as replacements for her parents."

His remark prompted them to pause momentarily. In this year, Alan was thirty-two years old, and Charlotte was thirty. They were too young for Eleanor to regard them as her parents. Besides, they had no interest in playing those roles.

"Oh, we will not be her parents," Alan said. His words were direct and clarifying. "At this point in her life, nobody could replace them. She has already built a history of loving and needing them. If she thought we were trying to be her parents, she would surely resent us."

"We will be her teachers and her advisors," Charlotte quickly added. It was, she knew, important for Gerald to understand the persons that they would be for his granddaughter.

Hearing her explanation, he permitted himself a broad smile. He was accompanying them through the long, shadow-tinctured hall out to a waiting car, their handsome

Bentley, and to the extraordinary May afternoon, itself another ascension flourishing around them.

"You will be wise counselors," he said. "You'll guide her to a realistic view of things. That is what she needs most of all."

As soon as she and Alan were seated in their car, which would bring them to their townhouse in Greenwich Village, she peered through the open window. With warmhearted intonations creating subtle intensities, she declared the very thought which had inspired their visit.

"I think we will teach her a new way to see."

Then it was that she noticed, as the car began a modulated departure—as if cars wisely instructed could make even departures charming—how pleased Gerald was with them, while he stood regarding their leave-taking. Her extemporary remark had, she hoped, drawn his keen mind toward an even firmer trust of them.

CHAPTER TWO
CONNECTEDNESS

When Charlotte and Alan first met her, Eleanor appeared to be a quiet, tentative girl trying to find her way toward a life both bracing and original. But they saw more than that, more than this eighteen-year-old girl who was becoming a young woman. In this first meeting with her, they noticed in Eleanor's sweet-natured affability a muted sorrow not unlike their own after the war, when they too had struggled to find their way back to the happiness their earlier experiences had promised them. That they no longer believed in the importance or the permanence of those promises did not diminish their willingness to guide this troubled girl toward her own realistic negotiations with life.

They found her reading quietly by the blue-rimmed well which was sequestered within a shadowed alcove of the late Mrs. Marnham's private rose garden. All in their seeing were harmonies of floribunda and hybrid teas, delicate rosemary and damask and blue-moon surfaces. Gerald brought them to her after he had concluded his first meeting with them in his study. No sooner had he observed them exchanging with his granddaughter a few affirmative remarks about the late spring and summery activities that, they hoped, she would enjoy—most often with Charlotte and sometimes with Alan, as well—than he was called back to his study to attend to some New York business that had followed him to this Newport retreat.

Alone with them now, Eleanor began opening her heart to them.

"I'm glad that you are going to be my friends," she said. "You will keep me from grieving away the summer." "Oh, we don't want you to grieve," Charlotte said as she gently took her hand as a close friend does when she is offering comfort and affection.

"Your grandfather wants you to be happy once again," Alan told her. Though he kept a respectful distance from her, his courtly manner and handsome assurance suggested that he had her well-being in mind. "Your mother and your father would want you to be happy, too." While accepting still Charlotte's gentle hand, Eleanor held her own right hand out to him as she drew him to her side. For a moment, flanked by the both of them, she seemed eased and accepting of the moment unfolding around them. Then, just as suddenly, she broke free of them.

"I wish I could be strong like them...like Father and Mother," she said. Her words were at first reluctant, as well as soft and tremulous. "I wish I could face life as bravely as they did."

She was standing now as when they had found her, pensive and willowy by the blue-rimmed well. They noticed the immaculate whiteness of her cotton dress. They noticed, too, that her weary unhappiness was muted, yet a palpable thing nonetheless.

At the moment just before they approached her, however, Eleanor had believed herself concealed by the rigor of her solitude. But in subtle witness they had arrived to notice how forlorn she appeared. They knew that she had returned to that place to hide this new onset of sorrow from them. Despite their having just met her, they felt that they perceived correctly the "idea" of this emerging young woman. They saw her as a bright and sometimes trammeled spirit yearning not merely to attend the world's progress, but to participate in its ambivalent nuances and sometimes in its emphatic gestures. Perceiving her so, they had determined almost instantly to be her friends. Though she had been cordial and for a moment had opened her heart to them, they sensed that she had not yet decided whether she should keep them at a distance. She leagued them, perhaps, with a generation too "grown-up" to understand the sorrows and secrets of her present life.

They thought it was a good time, here in the seclusion of the Marnhams' rose garden, to tell her that they knew something about the anguish she was experiencing.

"We've lost our dearest friends in the war," Charlotte said. "And Alan lost a cousin who had always been like a brother to him."

"We've seen so much death and misery," Alan explained. "We've learned with our own eyes that life can be very unfair."

"Our losses can become a bond for us," Charlotte said, "a genuine connectedness."

"We'll keep each other from falling into useless self-pity," Alan said. "Already, Charlotte and I are learning how to love the world again. We can show you, as well."

That they would help her claim her rightful share of happiness instantly lifted Eleanor's spirits. Upon witnessing her fleet smile, as hopeful as it was bright, Alan remembered as the flickering imagery of previous years, how life-loving and exuberant Eleanor appeared in the album of photographs which Gerald had allowed Charlotte and him to see at the conclusion of their meeting with him in his study. In those years all of the Marnhams spent part of their summers in Newport as a family whole and integral. In each photograph, Eleanor's glowing presence was already compelling. Her sprightly charm as a healthy girl of nine or ten was winning and impressive.

To observe her in this first hour of his knowing her, however, was to receive her as somebody different, if not completely separate—a reflection of a vital girl he saw in a photo and accurately remembered. Although nature had altered and clarified her lineaments and features, the very face and body and carriage she inhabited, all those amenities certainly left her intact. The imagery of herself in full bloom now told his apprehension none the less who she used to be and taught his eyes to receive her as a distinctive counterpart to the sunny girl in the photo he had seen only a half hour earlier. To his present glance, the sorrow that she held within herself was an additional layer of her existence. It revised the meaning of the photos, emphasizing their tentativeness.

Now, standing before their cautious solicitude, his and Charlotte's, and attending gratefully their sympathetic observation, Eleanor petitioned them for their understanding. The momentary hush, cloistered alone somewhere apart from the wind-stirred afternoon air, seemed itself like any other sensate being that showed an aptitude for listening. Only then did she reveal the truth of her situation.

"I don't want to go on needing Mother and Father," she said. "I loved them while they were alive, and I love them now as a memory. But I've had enough of death and all these months of mourning. I want life."

She paused, as if waiting for them to answer or rebuff the rebellious spirit of her complaint. Yet whatever words they cared to say, they held inside their circumspection, not a little impressed by her sudden flare of anger. So, she went forward, her questioning voice now more defensive than petitioning.

"Is it so wrong to want life?"

She was challenging them to gainsay the rightness of her inquiry. But, quickly noticing their courteous reticence, she hurried on to express the vibrant idea that gave to the timbre of her voice a harder edge and a tough-minded urgency.

"I want only life."

"And we'll be a part of it," Charlotte gently promised. Her enthusiasm rose discreetly at the prospect of rescuing this appealing, vulnerable girl. For she saw in that rescue a worthy calling for herself. A proper care could infuse her days with a profounder meaning that might sometimes surprise, if not altogether startle, her.

"We'll show you the way back to happiness," she reassured Eleanor, as though happiness were for herself and for Alan a recovered possibility—and a bit of wild luck and blessed chance.

"There will be days and days of happiness for you," Alan told her. His husky timbres ignited friendly capacities and whatever other guardian powers he possessed for dispelling a haunted girl's grief.

And so there were hours and days and weeks of

happiness to revive at first and then enthrall her. Now they drew her into festive occasions that flashed with quick time's waves and ripples. They took care always to guide her to the wholesome peers her family had in previous summers allowed her to befriend—hardy, keen-minded youths full-grown now and well-bred ethereal girls. The two of them sailed with her across the light of the sun welling beneath the tinted sea. With her they swam with acrobatic glee, all swift and gleaming spume-flecked motion. With a spate of life-loving friends (her trustworthy chums, along with Gerald's proven-loyal circle), they entered the colored velocity of a county fair. As agreeable chaperones in that late spring and summer of surprises, they dared her with them to climb her way to a perilous ridge. Just beyond a spotted raven's nest and twisted knots of grass, she—with them ascending adroitly—saw and heard, as for the first time because so proximate and actual, the rapid wingbeat of a black-backed gull. There, on that same ridge, they also observed the iridescent curve of cloud-flame cresting the hill above them and for one astonishing moment understood, as well, the symmetry and slant of the floating sky.

Through all these bracing occasions they restored her capacities for claiming the extraordinary possibility that was her young life unfolding. Yet they could dispel only intermittently the quiet sorrow that glimmered tensely. As if in spite of an hour's chance happiness, her sorrow revealed itself steadfast and intrinsic, like a palpable substance that was slowly burning away her soul.

Still, there grew around her, around this lost, lovely young woman who with their guardian powers assisting might after all be wonderfully rescued, hours and days and weeks that possessed the very spirit and pleasure by which she herself yearned to be possessed. Flourishing and supreme, here-and-now experience rose upon her senses and was so much more intensified than any mind-held happiness that from her hovering past could only be a remembered idea. Or so they at that time told themselves and told one another. For her joining with them in the full fervor of summer moments hurried her into a brave exhilaration. Then she knew a sweep of liberty whose startling rush and lift and emphasis were realistic measures of how much of her bright promise they were capable of saving.

That there was so much brightness to save, they perceived with casual-seeming attentiveness whenever Eleanor gave herself completely to the day's adventure. Observing her luminous form ascending a sun-glanced hill or riding the crest of wind-sheared waves or taming the curve of a billowing sail, they saw how fluently, given her will, her identity translated its differences. On those days she was for them and for others with a mind to notice as a lovely blossoming of nature, a flowering of crisp intention and act and emotion. The various meanings of herself became distilled through an array of nuances and emblems and increments that refused to be brought within the rule of arbitrary definition or any other narrowness.

Too often, though, there lingered, as if fastened about the tense capacities of her sorrow, a guilty reluctance to bring her own fervor to the festive weeks that they were providing. Each day now they regarded as a favorable sign of her wakening spirit every occasion when Eleanor, as if suddenly confident and self-governing, willed herself effortlessly to explore with them a day that made happiness seem, if not permanent, at least diverse and plausible. For that reason, they were heartened whenever she offered herself to the day's unexpected flare of surprise and to the promise, as well, of wildness not unlike adventure. This willowy image of a nearly blithe Eleanor brought them a quiet pleasure. For she appeared in those moments to be recovering all the happiness that she felt had been taken from her.

As they came to know her, Charlotte and Alan found Eleanor's poised reserve not without its singular charm and inspiring gravity. Her wind-tanned oval face, blonde hair, and clipped, New England intonations enhanced a quiet confidence and crisp directness. Her unmarred beauty and quickened sense of the deepest truth in things granted her a superb individuality. They were pleased that they were creating a special rapport with her. Whenever, with a convincing simplicity, they recounted life-loving exploits from their student days in Europe and, at the same time, related their particular joys in being new and promising, they noticed how tenderly Eleanor would glance from time to time toward each of them. With genuine elation, she listened to the splendid coherence of their narratives that, even in the rhythms of understatement, discovered their passionate natures and courageous willfulness. They had noticed, too, how apt and imaginative were the comments or inquiries she offered them as they told of their bold alliances with experience. Her well-schooled sociability identified her as winsome and wholly creditable. So impressed were they by the modulations within her of harmonies and tensions, a proper union of earthbound and ethereal, that they received as satisfying and inevitable the news that she shared their affection for Shakespeare's poems.

They had admired her sensitive commentary, for it mirrored their own reading of the poems even while imparting her own insights, which were often profound and sometimes original. One evening they heard her tell of her special affection for the one-hundred-sixth sonnet. Reading again and again the lyrical richness of this sonnet she most admired, she had thought it a witty surprise that

Shakespeare—or, rather, the persona through whom he spoke—should reproach himself for not achieving the mellifluous song he had meant to compose in honor of the one he loved. His words (he had declared) were inadequate to extol a being who surpassed all ordinary praise. In truth he required, so he believed, the divining eyes and tongues of the poetic chroniclers. He required, that is, a God-spun gift granting him the power to see and hear and describe as they had—the troubadours and minnesingers and trouvères of long ago. Theirs was a melodious art as invaluable as it was essential for presenting so sterling a reality as one's chosen lover.

It was the analogy implicit within the poem that the ancient verse chroniclers, singing the Platonic absolutes of fairest and best as they imaged the beloved coming into one's life, were not unlike the Old Testament prophets who, before them, had also seen, divined, and sung. Those prophets told us that Melchisedec and Moses, Enoch and Elijah, and Isaac and Jonah were foreshadowing figures of a coming Messiah. It was this analogy, perceiving one's lover as a god come to earth, a mystic equation of human- divine, which fascinated Eleanor. For to her mind, it gave to the beloved a power to eclipse whatever other divinity had promised to save her.

"That is, I think, what authentic love must always be," she remarked, her voice a warm, disarming grace. "It is a religion unto itself—with its own promises and rewards and tests of faith."

At the dinner table listening to her while they were alone there with her except for the butler and the maid attending them, Charlotte and Alan smiled. They were pleased at her words and found in her charming affirmation a very romantic young lady. They found her charming and romantic once more when with crisp inflections she recited Shakespeare's poem. Then they had observed the oblique light gently express her. A softer radiance (as if rising from within) belonged to her alone.

After that, they heard her tell of experiencing the flamingos during the summer when, as a nine-year-old girl with her parents and her Grandmother Marnham, she was traveling through the southern coast of France. On that August afternoon they were visiting the exotic Camargue, a picturesque region of shimmering lakes and sand dunes and reed beds. The Camargue was, as well, a park-like reserve sumptuous with billowing birds and their symphonic dissonances along the Grand Rhône that forks just north of Arles and, flowing east, spills into the tangy-scented Mediterranean.

It was there that for the first time Eleanor saw the flamingos. With delicate hues they were wading through the solacing waters of the étang de Vaccarès, the largest of the lakes in the Rhône Delta. Their tall and slender emphases possessed in the moment the reflecting waters they themselves were possessed by. The pink flush and black tips of their downward curving bills and roseate legs and plumage tinged the breeze-cooled air and fertile waters with a summer glow her yielding senses effortlessly savored. Intrigued, she noticed how, graceful and dexterous, they placed their heads beneath the mirroring lake. They pumped water through their bills and scooped backwards to catch with large, fleshy tongues small invertebrates and smaller plant matter that satisfied need or habit or instinct.

More remarkable to her roused apprehension were they on that afternoon than all the other picturesque birds arriving before her awareness as though to please her. There, she hurried as if to meet all of them at the threshold of the place that they were then inhabiting. Sovereign and proprietary over teeming, mottled wetlands, the black-winged stilts were extraordinary with legs red and long and plumage blending white and charcoal. In a flash, a flurry of energy and swift, irrevocable rhythms, they picked incessantly at their prey, all the while consuming them. Far from her still, yet no less astonishing, tall and private and disdainful on a grassy islet, a sleek-blue, wily heron moved with solitary deliberation into waiting, restless waters. Masterfully, it held its outstretched neck forward and angled down stiffly the sharp accuracy of its bill, just before piercing through the silver sheen of an ample fish.

Closer now, after with her parents and her grandmother she passed through a sequestered alcove and wended her way toward glimmering marshes, she saw the crouching brightness of bitterns. They—all of them with buffy colors—were active hunters in those reedy locations. Closer yet, with her parents and her grandmother she passed now by a green, luminous field discovered only on the easterly path they, a moment earlier, had left behind them. Here, frisky egrets showed pale yellow bills and lacy plumes the color of snow. While they foraged, proficient and erect, they held their wiry necks tightly coiled before striking. When she and her parents and her grandmother reached a low, ferny embankment, she saw—quite suddenly, there in the ripples and sunspots of the lake—a green-winged teal. With dark rufous head, legs gray and agile, and small, delicate bill, it was dabbling at the swaying surfaces of water, the better to lift up tiny fish.

How clearly nature revealed to her eyes that day its casual betrayals. She recognized in its splendor a darker intimation about the danger within its beauty—an intimation which her keen mind and the early promptings of her intuition had already taught her. That beauty could so naturally destroy did not alter her acceptance of the scene or taint the pleasure that sang to her heart because the earth contained such flux and entanglement and profusion.

It was the surprise and mystery of beauty which intrigued her. Always, beauty suggested that it was something other than its outward appearance at first declared. The mystery and its promise called her soul to all the places she cared to remember: to art and music and books and to those remarkable human beings, a few, who mattered more to her than any other promise.

Now it was that she saw again the enthralling flamingos. But this time they were navigating waves upon waves of sun-caressed clouds. The pink flame of their wings was a flush or flare upon the floating sky. Just then in their spiraling ascensions she saw them, momentarily, even as they disappeared before her approving witness inside wind-glanced circumferences of clouds. The heaping layers of low cumulus and vaporous trails of cirrus were all cerulean sky-tint and yellow ocher ambiance in alliance with cream whites and grays and the glow of alizarin. Exhilarated beyond decorum's permissible expression, its nuanced reserve the signifying quality of her class, she was running now as if she were a girl enchanted. Flinging herself free of all restriction, she ran toward the dazzle of flamingos and sky-hills and cloud-waves. Her intention was to follow so admirable a flight of birds until every one of them had vanished. All the while, she cried out the words declaring herself to them—to the peerless birds who knew the secrets of the sky and cloud and wind.

"I want to," she cried out. "I want to."

Her voice was an emphatic declaration as much as a tremulous lament.

She had felt a restraining hand, elegantly gloved and feminine, placing itself on her shoulder. Only then did she pause in her earth-held flight. With surprise she turned to observe her mother's cool serenity express itself in a loving smile and to hear quiet, accurate words guiding her back to her proper self.

"What is it that you want, Eleanor?" she gently asked while studying with pensive directness the complicated individuality of this beautiful daughter. "What are you running toward?"

She noticed all of them now. Her father and her grandmother were arriving just behind her mother to stand before her. Because they apparently enjoyed the charm of her secret yearning made suddenly palpable, they smiled through their own curious inquiry of this altogether unexpected Eleanor.

"Tell us. Do," her father advised. His deep resonant voice was frugal of emotion. "Tell us what you want."

She could not, in the first moments of her seeing them, locate within her disarranged attention the necessary words that would shape an adequate answer. The surprise of herself openly declared and of their quiet contemplation of her stranger manifestation inhibited whatever exuberance and spontaneity she had for once freely summoned while in their presence.

"I want to be like them...like the flamingos," after a moment's reflection she heard herself saying. "I want to be lost and then find my way back."

Her father, still watching her closely, allowed his smile to stay, though almost imperceptibly. He regarded her innocent openness as no small merit in her favor.

That time Grandmother Marnham, enhancing the propriety that had shaped her, glanced affectionately at her. With a grown-up's voice of counsel, she spoke words which suggested her wise balance.

"Those birds are not lost," she said, trying to be helpful. "They know where they are going."

At her grandmother's attempt to revise her fanciful perceptions, she frowned.

"They may become lost sometimes," she replied. She did not care for her grandmother's words that to her mind seemed condescending and even imperious. "Everyone becomes lost, at least once in a while."

"Well, don't *you* try to become lost," her mother said, regarding her daughter's startling wish with new unease. "Not in the clouds or anywhere else, my dear."

She took her hand now, as though she meant to remind her of the emerging bond between them, where nobody should ever become lost. Then, guiding her return to the path the four of them had been traversing, she imparted with carefully modulated finality the words that would hurry them away from an unhappy subject.

"When you become lost," she said, "you may never find your way back."

Hearing Eleanor, nine years later, tell of her exhilaration before the splendid flight of the flamingos, Charlotte and Alan perceived in her that evening a charming ingenuousness. Her disposition was poetic and idealistic. In their eyes, she appeared to be a bright girl capable of declaring her own spirited challenge to the world. Perhaps, when she called out to the flamingos her wish to follow their journey, she meant to subvert whatever hesitancy or reticence within herself made her vulnerable and might defeat her. It was this willingness to share graciously the truths of herself that endeared her to both of them. By interpreting a sonnet and describing a sky become radiant with colorful birds, she had revealed who she was and what she believed and how, with attractive and intricate subtexts, she embraced romantic ideals.

"She's very romantic," Alan said after he and Charlotte had retired to their suite of rooms in the Marnham home. "That can be a good thing, if she learns to use it well." "She'll need more than that," Charlotte said. "She has to see the world for what it really is."

Then, because Eleanor's untouched loveliness had

ignited the memory of his earliest passion for his wife, he cast his heated glance upon Charlotte. With wily intimation, she met that glance as if she were looking upon a new and satisfying lover. For Eleanor's romantic exuberance had also stirred her appetite. Roused with a fervor they had not known since before the war, she and Alan would influence this night to become one of life's happier occasions.

During the weeks that followed, this complicated matter of recovering her authentic presence in the world gave Eleanor a special pleasure. For, just before she entered this period of self-recovery, she had disengaged herself from the singular identity she had been cultivating with the assistance of her parents, her teachers, and her own will. Not only had she lost the often radiant and sometimes too-delicately pensive girl her mirror's imagery had allowed her to peruse—the unique and hopeful person whose identity she had been creating all through the earlier years of her life. But she had also lost the more recent imagery of an emerging young woman as well. That person had been herself no less, though a familiar stranger still who dwelled most often as in secret within her impassioned thought. Lately, she had been an imaginative and sometimes ingenious girl who was learning to negotiate effectively with the world even when she had to endure long separations from her parents. When they—Kevin and Rebecca Farrell—died, she appeared at first to turn away from this promising, strong-minded young woman that she was learning to be. Disarranged by her grief, she had neglected the upbuilding of her character. Yet, after the first weeks of this journey with Charlotte, she found herself accepting the disciplines of a new, authentic life. The person she was becoming was as contemporary as she was studious and altruistic.

At the close of her sessions with her psychiatrist and right after her graduation, she had returned with her grandfather to the coherent splendors of his Federal-Revival home along Ocean Drive. That home was a stately amplitude of twenty-five acres that each year taught her, with nuances subtly different from any she had before experienced, the bracing freedoms of the sea's crisper breezes and of full-flowering fields and congregant majestic trees. All in the comfort of her seeing was married to a green world nurtured and enhanced by the inspired design of her Grandmother Marnham and by that formidable woman's efficient cadre of landscape architects and gardeners. When her doctors advised her that it would be better for her to continue her studies at her grandfather's home in Newport rather than to begin her Bryn Mawr program, she had not protested, even though she knew that she would miss the four Bryn Mawr-enrolled friends of whom she had grown very fond during the years she had spent with them at Miss Porter's.

Possibly, her reluctance to begin her program there derived from her intuitive awareness that acceding to her grandfather's plan for her would fortify whatever harmony she could compose in her relations with him. Or an uneasy insight persuaded her that, by remaining at home, she would elude another fall into despair. Away from the solacing environment which her grandfather's home had always been for her and away from the stewards and keepers of his household whose familial presence she had come to cherish, she would surely fall into despair. Possibly, it was that apprehension which influenced her to continue her studies at home. Or, more likely, it was her understanding that, because of her losing her parents, she could no longer return to the girlhood innocence of her peers. In every other respect, those young ladies were like her, a well-born blend of straitlaced and spirited.

Or, most probable of all, she recognized that in this year of home study, she would more freely navigate experience—its prismatic diversity and pleasing capaciousness. Even while under the watchful guidance of Charlotte and Alan and while in their company, she would frequently visit art galleries and scientific exhibits and attend theatre and opera, chamber concerts and symphonies. She would also attend university lectures pertaining to philosophy and mathematics and offer her charitable services to the needy.

Whether each of these possibilities influenced her acceptance of a schedule which would keep her away from Bryn Mawr, an environment which would also enable her to thrive, or one possibility more than any of the others, she could not, even in those moments when she paused long enough in her busy schedule to consider the rewards and liabilities of so choosing, tell herself with assurance that she knew. So tenuous was her certainty of all that the life unfolding about her signified—its ellipses and ambiguities testing nonetheless her steadfastness and her courage.

That her grandfather had asked Charlotte Aubray, a specialist in modern languages, to be her instructor was all to the good—the good, that is, of her continuing evolution as an eighteen-year-old girl becoming both educated and aesthetic. For Charlotte would help her to hone her knowledge of French and German as well as Italian and Spanish. She would also share with her the memory of having lived in Europe for many of her early years. Just as important, she would show her how to make her way in the rugged world.

Even in the first weeks of their relationship as teacher and pupil, Charlotte taught her how to make her life useful. She influenced her to respect the earth she inhabited and to be, through positive actions and lifelong learning, its prudent benefactor. In these first weeks, she persuaded her to translate herself through the good works which accurately represented her strong-minded personhood. Exuberantly, with Charlotte as a knowing guide, she pursued new involvement in ecological programs, including the protection of the forests in southeastern Rhode Island and the preservation of the islands and wildlife of Narragansett Bay. She was involved as well in social services on behalf of handicapped children, the elderly poor and the homeless, and the unemployed who needed retraining in marketable skills. She continued to read biographies of leaderly activists such as Julia Ward Howe, Jane Addams, and Florence Nightingale. In this season which she regarded as her convalescence from grief, she renewed her affinity for worthwhile occupation. She sensed that her life was once more becoming an expression of using time well.

She was aware that Charlotte was guiding her away from her uneasy, problematic self and into a formidable home-schooling that would prepare her for her college days. That Charlotte had taught young ladies at the exclusive Newbury School was all to the good—the good, that is, of her grandfather's pragmatic aims. Now that she had left behind Miss Porter's School and was postponing Bryn Mawr for a year, he wanted her to make a friend of Charlotte. With this gifted teacher as her mentor, her grandfather had reminded her before he embarked on a series of business trips that would take him out of the country, she would learn to choose and to appreciate the gifts which the world kept offering her. She would also learn to fulfill all the obligations her acceptance of those gifts, in good conscience and with fair-minded reciprocity, entailed.

It brought her a special pleasure to communicate the whole day long with this remarkable teacher exclusively in French or Italian, German or Danish or Spanish. She was conscious that each day not only intensified her disciplined aptitudes, but also prepared her for a life in the wider world. That experience, she imagined, would be even more adventurous and creative than the everyday reality which now spun its ambivalence around her. It was always challenging and sometimes surprising to collaborate with remarkable Charlotte. With infinite variety, this astute teacher accompanied her to the further discovery of her immense and untested possibilities. In ways even more effective than those her previous schooling had allowed her, she was learning how to be the maker of herself and the shaper of her destiny. Out of her best capacities and with nearly spontaneous symmetry, she was fashioning the unique being who was her evolving self.

So it was, in the full consciousness of her evolution, that for the next weeks she learned from each day's challenging studies and altruistic endeavors the virtues of maintaining an intellectual rigor toward herself, especially in tense or formidable circumstances. She also learned the virtues of helping those who are poor or sick or abandoned in old age to a lonely dying. Though it was not Charlotte alone who challenged and guided her to enlarge her capacities for achieving her worthiest aspirations, the influence of this woman worked, nevertheless, its affirmative powers upon her. Within a few weeks of their meeting as teacher and pupil, they quickly achieved a natural rapport. Charlotte became for her a gentle advisor, a discreet confidante, and a superb mentor. Not only did she draw from her a flawless performance as a multi-lingual student of the world's varied cultures. But she also accompanied her with quick-witted and ingrained precision through advanced programs in philosophy, biology, and calculus.

More than that, in these weeks with Charlotte as her guide, there occurred during the many Samaritan visits they paid to the sick or poor, as well as to the aged or injured, the clearest evidence of her progress away from the sometimes impulsive and often self-absorbed girl her privileged background had influenced her to be. True it was that, within the first few weeks of becoming reacquainted with the less inward and more altruistic facets of her character, she had drawn always upon her capacities to help those far less fortunate than she. And true again that, while on beneficent visits to the needy and in the presence of Charlotte's authentic empathy toward the suffering and the needy, she had acquitted herself effectively. With the quietude of a humble nurse, she had administered the corporal works of mercy that had brought her to the working-class suburbs which stood, unobtrusive and ordinary, beyond the visible rims of Newport. But she had never completely entered the experience of sharing her humanness with these struggling members of her species who often, despite their hardships, maintained a proud and undaunted resilience.

Now, during the later Samaritan visits of this first season of her recovery, she discovered within herself a profound sympathy for the anguished and afflicted and abandoned. There grew in her a genuine desire to do all that she could to help them. In this period, she often brought her solacing presence to a dying, tubercular girl of twenty whose stoic resignation intensified an ethereal loveliness. On other days she encouraged new self-determination in an embittered war veteran who—at twenty-four—was learning to walk again, assisted as he was by a prosthetic leg. Quietly moved by his plight, she persuaded her grandfather to finance his enrollment into law school. When this young hero earned his law degree, there would be a place for him within the legal department of the Marnham Steel Corporation. In more recent days, she worked for many hours helping to paint and to furnish three large brownstones, so that the children and the widows of firefighters and policemen killed in the line of duty could make comfortable homes in attractive, modern apartments. To these afflicted human beings and to others like them, she also offered with her enlightened teacher the sustenance of food and clothing and empathetic words.

There were, at this time, many other frail or fallible persons whose spirits revived because of her presence. As if each time were a revelation meant for her alone, there came upon her awareness the truth that each of these suffering and broken and needy belonged to herself. They belonged, that is, to the human family she represented. Her heart's new knowledge and the clarity of accurate recognition taught her to receive them, in the very hour she was assisting them, as upright and worthy relations.

In these early weeks of summer, both Charlotte and Alan were surprised and very pleased by her spontaneous expressions of sympathy and by the efficacy of her Samaritan deeds. They began to believe that this rigorous period of displacing her grief was making Eleanor a most capable human being.

Nor were they alone in noticing Eleanor's admirable influence upon a scene of tattered hopes or painful illness, irrevocable loss or careworn frailty. Gerald, having returned briefly from his latest business trip abroad, also observed the favorable signs of his granddaughter's new-found maturity. He had, on two occasions, assisted Charlotte and Eleanor in their visits to the sick and the needy and never failed, in the diplomatic stillness of his accurate perceptions, to appreciate the girl's hard-edged and unhesitant confrontation with the dark blight of existence from which her own life's safe amenities had shielded her. How startling it was, at first, to witness so radical a change, even in her appearance. Gone was the grieving, introverted girl with the blonde glow upon the curly ringlets of her flowing hair and a trouble-haunted intensity within her blue eyes. Gone too was the dissatisfied girl with a hint of hauteur in her perfect profile and the hint of bitterness within her genteel smile and the sometimes-rigid tension in her feminine gait. In their stead was a young woman with blonde hair pulled back to form a sensible coil at the nape of her neck. With steady, encouraging eyes and determined profile...pursed lips and assertive gait, she hurried to meet the sober and problematic world.

"She is becoming a very promising young woman," Gerald remarked to Charlotte, one afternoon in early July.

They were quickening their pace along the winding flagstone path which guided them in their brisk afternoon walk past terraced banks rising one behind another and an artfully graded lawn that sloped into a meadow of midsummer's flowers. All in their seeing were orange butterfly weed and red-violet musk mallows...gold and white oxeye daisies and sapphire blue Douglas irises. The path brought them past long, precise hedgerows and the granite wall that directed the eye agreeably toward a wind-stirred sea. It brought them, as well, down the bluestone steps hugging the rugged bluff and onto the tawny sands of the beach. Before arriving to meet those steps, they had smoothly descended from the hill-top perch which held Gerald Marnham's ample and pristine Newport home seven hundred feet from the shore.

That Gerald, during his bracing walk with Charlotte, would remark upon Eleanor's progress seemed, at the moment, appropriate and pertinent. For as they accelerated their pace, the better to attain the clearest expression of their keen vitality, they chanced to glimpse Eleanor seated supple and erect on a splendid bay-colored Arabian horse. She was cantering in the palpable distance to their left, along undulating verdant land that scanned amidst a wide array of hills a grove of early-blooming lilac trees. Their tints of rose-pink and azure and amethyst were swaying, graceful and submissive, before the will of the wind. Swaying, too, were cream-white flowering cherries and the flourishing golden rain trees. How poised and adept she appeared to their seeing. With the assistance of a professional horse trainer, she was guiding a limber girl of ten and her eight-year-old brother—a wiry, athletic lad—to ride with the buoyant confidence they'd gained in many, careful weeks of instruction. (They two, lad and sister, were mounted favorably on short and hardy chestnut-brown Caspian ponies.)

"She has become, if not altogether new, then surely

someone whose differences make her capable of surprising you," Charlotte remarked.

At this time, she persuaded Gerald to pause with her momentarily. From afar, they observed Eleanor bring patience and empathy to the lessons which she and the retired, yet still agile, jockey were offering to these strong-hearted children. Their parents, who were slowly convalescing in a Boston hospital, had suffered grievous burns in a fire that had injured sixty other persons and had consumed the textile factory in nearby Middletown. There, they had worked long and arduous hours.

"How right you are," Gerald said.

He was pleased that his granddaughter continued to thrive and pleased, also, that she had opened her heart so generously to those two sturdy children who were learning not only how to ride a Caspian pony, but also how to prevail in spite of misfortune and disappointment. (Each of us must learn that lesson and keep on learning it—even a girl as privileged as Eleanor. So, he remarked to Charlotte, whose gentle smile suggested that she agreed with this conventional wisdom which his understatement kept from sounding too prosaic. Still smiling, she went on watching the four riders hurry into the nebulous, waiting distance.)

"That is one young woman who will never lose her mystery," she declared after a momentary reflection upon Eleanor's poise. "I need not remind you, I know, that a tremendous thing has been happening to her these many weeks. She's discovering some of her best capacities and some of her obligations, too."

"Ah, yes, *there's* the adventure, and she's testing herself in it."

So remarking, Gerald—with resilient Charlotte keeping effective pace—hurried forward to the sun-dappled sands of the beach. Standing in closer proximity to the restless and shimmering sea, they were conscious of the serenities of floating clouds (cumulus and feathery), an azure-bright sky, and the gold-flecked horizon. Now they heard even more clearly the crash of spumy, viridian waves upon the whiteness of glistening rocks and felt breeze-tossed mist upon their skin. In the same moment, they saw a host of gray-brown gulls, accurate and wily and steadfast. Each of these birds—with a broad ring of black color within its bill—was scooping plump mackerel from prodigal, indifferent waters.

That Eleanor's adventure should involve not only her Samaritan efforts, but also her cultivation of the privileged society into which she was born, Charlotte was certain. But on that day she did not mention her plan to enhance the education by which she and Alan were assisting Eleanor in her self-willed transformation. There would be time, she knew, for her to do the thing that she believed must be done if Eleanor was to make her way in the wider world. That Eleanor was cultivating a genuine selflessness as well as a disciplined scholarship was all to the good. Her conduct, with its assured decorum and genteel reserve, would please even the most austere dowagers of her class. But one day, before she turned to the protective atmosphere of Bryn Mawr, both she and Alan planned to introduce her to the discreet intricacies of her sensuality. Only then would she make her way effectively in an ambivalent world.

CHAPTER THREE
MÉNAGE À TROIS

1

Alan planned all of it, this ménage à trois which would draw them into a labyrinth of his and Charlotte's own devising. With hushed elation and restless need, Eleanor consented to whatever ingenuities they might impose upon its wayward design. That, in these many weeks, they had come to know each other well was all to the good—the good, that is, of their liberated purposes. How bracing it was to be, as if at the very same moment, roused by desire newly wakened and with solacing ease confronted. On those occasions when with them she was enjoying some free time away from her studies and her community service, they were careful to bring her to a group of her peers. Always, she was aware that they were discreetly watching her from a distance while allowing her and seven or eight of her peers a latitude for navigating a responsible individuality. Because she was so often enclosed within this group of her peers, she could experience a promising intimacy with Alan and Charlotte only by an indirection that searches out the unobtrusive path or quiet alcove or private arbor.

At first, she had to content herself with their presence obliquely, as if she were attracted primarily to the group and not to them especially. All during those splendid days when extemporaneous circumstance or summer occasions carefully planned by others availed them, they held themselves toward her as casual allies neither predominant nor ancillary to her engagement with the hardy, callow youths and lissome, emerging young women from backgrounds similar to her own. No matter that they were for these gregarious occasions in the company of her friends' parents. Affable and upright with them, they appeared to enjoy their roles as chaperones both gentle and careful. While they were there, permitting themselves at times to join with the parents the mingling of keen-eyed youths and understated young ladies who had been her friends for several years, Alan and Charlotte were for her a charismatic influence. Their quick-witted repartee within the group and their good-natured fellowship eased her excited senses. She was conscious of being on the brink of experience altogether different and momentous.

Her being with the two of them alone brought her an even larger measure of happiness. During these extraordinary days, she knew the heartbeat hum of excitement. As if spellbound, she experienced the joy of being prodigiously alive, because for her they were spirit-driven earth-mates...full-bodied sensualities. How wonderful it was to be with each of them even obliquely, while they—as if they were her exuberant friends rather than her dutiful chaperones—went cantering along the meandering sands of a private beach on Arabian horses, bay or black or chestnut. The wind-raveling spray of afternoon breakers was a cool, luxuriant touch to warm skin and pulsing motion. Wonderful as well it was to enter the colored velocity of a county fair and on a visit to a picturesque farm to ride on a wagonload of sweet-scented hay. With frolicsome ease in sight of a sun-tinted sea, they also picnicked at the foot of rugged gray cliffs in Falmouth. The steadfast verticality of those cliffs scaled cloud-dwelling altitudes for miles upward.

Then there came those times when she was alone with Alan. The sublime chance of their unanticipated encounter was a sign or harbinger of happiness that would be theirs to claim in sequestered awareness.

One time, the very first time which was different from all those times when she consented to the group's priorities so that she might be near this man who cast his spell upon her, he found her alone, pensive and ethereal at the entrance of a sumptuous grove on the ample grounds of her grandfather's home. There, he met her with a smooth courtesy and asked whether he might join her. After she agreed, he sauntered with her into the light-reflected shadows that lent mystery to the grove. Together, they entered breeze-stirred and fragrant symmetries of lilac trees white, lavender and crimson; orange-red rowans and translucent green aspens; and comely mimosas with feathery leaves and powdery gold flowers. As in a dream, she strolled with him along a wide, cleared path while they spoke of many things—music and art, poetry and aspirations and freedom. On the rim of a sudden stillness between them and in the heat of his passion, his body grew taut and his breathing became tighter. Momentarily, he cupped her lovely face with his rugged hands. Then with gentle proficiency he drew her willowy grace to the lithe muscularity that was himself and planted upon her lips a tender kiss. With shy reticence she drew away as quickly as she could. But the stillness that came to watch with him her graceful movement told her that her warm blue eyes and warm, delicate flesh left none the less their spell upon him. He would not on that afternoon take her, though the intensity of his gaze and the warm touch of his hands suggested his need for her. Here, within a sheltered June grove on the Marnhams' ample property, he would not yet allow his body the invigorating privilege of taking her. He meant first of all to befriend her. Because she was a demure and well-born young lady, he would have to waken gradually her sexual need of him.

Several days later, while they were held still to the Marnhams' ocean-front home, they happily met, this time by a careful design of their making. Her excited senses were roused by him more easily now in the sumptuous harmonies of a rose garden, all else in their seeing gold and cream-velvet textures and profusions of floribunda and hybrid teas. Even then he would not take her. Instead, he permitted himself only the muted pleasure of intimating how much he enjoyed being with her. As she paused at a blue-rimmed well, she received with easy elation his quiet words. In her eyes he appeared more handsome than ever before. Now she told him that her need of him was growing more essential.

"I'm glad you like me," she said. Her confession was as direct as it was extemporaneous and therefore more natural than his remark. "It makes my liking you so much grander."

Nor (she perceived) would he take her on a later afternoon when he had found her alone in the shimmering meadow of silver grasses that hurried toward a yellow ocher horizon, verdurous as well and luminescent. The delicate grays and violets of low stratus clouds were floating in the sun-washed sky. She was seated poised and accurate at her artist's easel in a blue-mist summer frock and broad-brimmed white linen hat. There, in that solacing privacy a quarter of a mile from the Marnhams' main house, though on her grandfather's property nonetheless, sweet-scented grasses and flowering trees were softly swaying around her. That day, she was surprised from her pastime by his being suddenly and marvelously there for her. So pleased was she by his having come freely to her, that she caressed his sun-bronzed face with the fair coolness of her hand.

Even then he would not take her. Now, though, he could see that her desire was as a fuse disarranging in an altogether new way her uneasy heart.

As if he wanted to excite through his absence her need of him, he withdrew from her company for a week. On each of these days she saw him from a far distance, as she often had seen him in the weeks which had too swiftly passed. He was working with teams of architects, masonry and landscape contractors, and tree movers to re-create her grandfather's large estate. So it was that in his absence Charlotte brought her once more into a confederacy of energetic and life-loving peers. These bright young people (all of them eighteen or nineteen) shared with her and Charlotte, as well as with their parents, days and days of swimming and sailing and water-skiing. But not even her friends' exuberance or their parents' smooth hosting of each occasion or Charlotte's charming anecdotes could allay her longing for Alan.

One evening during this cycle of days and nights

when Alan was hard at work and not available to either of them, Charlotte allowed her to sleep with her. Alan was in his study, busy with the revisions of architectural plans and engineering charts. It was not the first time that Charlotte and Eleanor had spent the night together, as though they were sisters bringing comfort to each other during the tentative fury of a lightning storm or the uneasy aftermath of a disappointing day. Tonight, though, while they enjoyed their solacing nearness, Charlotte drew from her the words which revealed her more-than-ordinary feelings for Alan as well as for her.

"You love Alan the way a woman loves a man she wants to sleep with."

Charlotte caressed her as she spoke the words. She was obviously pleased. More than that, her smile suggested that the thought of this inexperienced girl's loving Alan roused her.

"I love him so much," Eleanor confessed. "I want him to love me, as well."

"Ah, my dear," Charlotte said. "You must say what you mean. You want Alan to make love to you."

"Yes, I do. Very much."

"Then he will be very pleased," Charlotte said. "He has a large appetite and needs both of us."

Now, because their words had not only resolved her unease, but had also promised them new pleasures, they spent the hour before they fell into sleep speaking with sisterly briskness of the new fashions in hats and dresses, of the extensive travel they were planning, and of their experiences piloting a plane. Although neither Charlotte nor Eleanor mentioned Alan again that night, Eleanor perceived very clearly that this French woman whom she found altogether intriguing was as excited as she that the three of them would soon share the same bed and their sensuality.

2

"I can't bear to be separated from you," Eleanor told Alan when he was free to enjoy a day with her. With unresolved contentment, she accepted now his fevered embrace of her while she whispered her plaintive words. They were standing in the lush privacy of the Marnhams' rose garden that had become for them a favorite meeting place. "There is no happiness for me in any place where you are not."

She had hurried to him after Charlotte told her that they three would be spending the weekend in the home of their Nantucket friends. Those cosmopolitan persons were visiting their relatives on the West Coast. Soon Alan, Charlotte, and she would be joining the festive lightheartedness that was theirs to possess while they swam in prismatic, late June waters or sunned on colorful fabrics in the exuberant light of the pleasing afternoon. At last languorous and temporarily blissful, they would loll in the comfort of canvas-backed chairs. The coil and curve of beach-sand would be a warm intimacy against their leaning, outstretched hand gathering it to the soothed touch.

So Charlotte promised her.

Without revealing to Charlotte her veiled purpose, she hurried away on the pretext that she had promised to help Mrs. Appleton, their primary housekeeper, select flowers from one of her grandfather's splendid gardens. Together, they would arrange them in delicate vases for the dinner table as well as for the rooms where four guests from New York would be staying overnight. She hurried away with a rapturous heart, though not at first. Instead, she lingered on the beach with Charlotte and a few of the Aubrays' poised, summery friends who were passing through on their way to Bar Harbor in Maine. She waited until Alan arrived. Within the liveliness of that affable circle, he looked suntanned and lithe and accurate. The stylized confidence of Charlotte, standing near him while they conversed with two dark-haired women, was to her eyes an attractive counterpoint enhancing Alan's quicksilver singularity.

When he turned to greet her, though, she received him casually. The modulations of her joy, made cautious so that others might not witness her wakened need of him, were stays against confusion. With correspondent and still mute elation, she noticed his surreptitious glance a half hour afterward summoning her to the garden behind the main house. Patiently, she waited there until he arrived, comforting herself with the thought that twice before the garden had served well their desire to be alone, together.

There, at that clandestine meeting in a fragrant garden, she saw most clearly, with an unexpected awe rousing her appetite, the intensity of her love for him. So essential on that afternoon did he appear to her and so urgent was her love for him, that she paused. She felt a momentary compunction before the prospect of freely enjoying the pleasure of his love during all the summer days that were left to them. Her need of him, she had to admit, exceeded her affection for Charlotte. But the thought that she might have Charlotte's friendship as well as Alan's love recalled her to herself, to the already hardened part of her nature that resisted hesitancy and convention and the sentimental.

"We're going to have a first-rate time together," he said. Once more he drew her willowy radiance into his embrace while he eased her disquiet at their having been separated for the long week just passed. "We're just beginning."

Her happiness, now under his spell, brightened at so

auspicious a thought. Yet she consented nonetheless to a decorous protest.

"But I want to be with you all the time."

Appreciating the absolute charm of her, he gently laughed. "Nobody is together all the time," he said. "The world's a very busy place and occasionally needs us for other purposes."

Now it was she who kissed him, the light pressing of her lips upon his own a delicate sensuality...an exciting subtlety.

"I don't care about the world," she declared a moment later. Happily, she lost herself in the enclosure that was his embrace of her. He was the longed-for sanctuary.

He beamed, while with courtly assurance guiding her toward the privacy of a flowering gazebo.

"Well, then, be happy, for Heaven's sake. Right now," he said. His voice was smoky with his roused pleasure at her touch. "Because we are together and because we have days and days of summertime before us."

He did not take her even on that afternoon, harnessing through self-command the raw intensity of his passion for her. He was, at the same time, aware that Mrs. Appleton—the housekeeper—or their New York friends or a crew of diligent gardeners or butlers or Sommers, Gerald's driver, might by chance come there and discover them. Besides, he had already devised the episode by which, with Charlotte as an ardent partner, they could freely—and in a setting as secure as it was romantic— consummate their love. The three of them were, he told her, in mind and spirit already married to each other.

Through this idea, a convincing belief asserting their bond with each other, he came to persuade her of the rightness of his plan. At a picturesque home within the secluded seaport of Nantucket, they would—in fragrant privacies and without the Church's approving seal or any other legal document permitting them—celebrate the marriage of their bodies to one another. On that night they would activate their own personal laws. That they, by so doing, would at the same time subvert narrow convention and protect themselves from the public's accusing eyes would serve well to enhance their mutual pleasure.

"How clever you are," she said just before kissing him once more, exhilarated and breathless.

"There are many ways to have an adventure," he told her. His full, sensual lips now caressed the exquisite lobe of her right ear. "We've found the proper day for this one to begin."

In Nantucket, Eleanor shared with Alan and Charlotte the quickened pleasures of sailing on the sun-mottled waters of Vineyard Haven and swimming with a smooth swiftness at Tisbury Town Beach. Assertive and reliable, they also paddled on the sinuous propulsion of the

Deerfield River in nearby Zoar.

One afternoon she walked with them in the tawny glow of Tisbury Town Beach, musing about the capable lives they were then inhabiting. They mused as well about their plans for the future. Still they knew the tangy scent of the sea. Still the splash and ripple of massive waters broke upon the shore. Still the slant light of the sun shone upon the beach like flame or phosphorescence.

"I want to help the world even in some small way," she told the two who were, with her, in a reflective mood as they sauntered barefoot along the soft, coiling textures of cool, silvery sand. Their white shirts and slacks billowed in the breeze and granted them a temporary emphasis upon the afternoon. "I want to study medicine so that I can make life better for the poor people in our country."

Charlotte, hearing her words, imbued as they were by pragmatic altruism, studied her with special interest. This was the first time that Eleanor declared so openly her belief that she had come into the world to make it a better place.

"You're aiming very high and very nobly, too," Charlotte observed.

Her favorable response was altogether genuine, though carefully muted by all that her war-time experience had taught her about human nature.

"Do your part to make the world better, without

believing that you are performing miracles."

"Oh, I won't be a miracle worker," Eleanor said. Lighthearted that day, she laughed at the thought. "But I plan to be helpful."

"Being helpful can be a good thing," Alan said, "if you can make your goodness wily and resourceful as well."

"Does goodness have to be wily?"

"Yes," he answered her. "We live in a rugged world."

As the three of them sauntered along the beach, she noticed all the while, though merely scanning the looming distance to the right of her, the roar and rush of spume-flecked waves leaping and echoing with sonorous powers. She noticed, too, that her optimistic words had brought to Alan as well as to Charlotte a momentary stillness and a subtle frown. But it was Alan who now advised her that neither her goodness nor her helpfulness would alter the world's marauding instincts.

"Don't imagine that you will cure the world of its bad habits," he said. "It will take plenty of courage simply to offer your good deeds to a world that is so problematic and dangerous."

Now, with a clipped intensity harnessing his bitterness, he spoke of the casual depredation roiling across the globe.

In Germany Adolf Hitler had begun, through a

political uprising in Munich, his insidious forays against democracy. In Italy Benito Mussolini was governing through a Fascist-controlled Parliament. By means of that Fascist organization, he arranged the kidnapping and the assassination of his primary opponents, including the Socialist leader Giacomo Matteotti. In Asia Minor Turks and Greeks had recently clashed in decimating warfare. In China there raged a relentless war between the forces of General Wu Pei-fu in Peking and Chang Tsu-Lin's Manchurian Army. Within a few hours their brute combat claimed seven thousand lives.

In America the lynching of innocent black men in Chicago led to six days and nights of rioting. Because of its fear and hatred of foreigners, the United States denied its freedom to immigrants from Russia, Poland, and Italy. In America's southern states the Ku Klux Klan carried forward its murderous policies against African Americans, Jews, and Catholics. The Presidential Administration of the recently deceased Warren Harding had tarnished itself with the scandal of Harding's cronies, including the Secretary of the Interior and millionaire businessmen, misappropriating three huge oil reserves on government land in Teapot Dome, Wyoming, that had been set aside for the use of the Navy. Even more grievous in America, poverty blighted the lives of hardworking farmers; and Indians, African Americans, and Mexican Americans lived marginal existences as their nation's disinherited.

"The most affirmative philosopher confronting all these harms might well wonder how any of us could find a way to redress even a small portion of the wrongdoing."

"I know what is in the world," Eleanor said. "Both of you have helped me to understand it in a new way."

She paused. She was searching for words which would redefine her perspective without denying Alan's review of the world's troubles.

"All that you have said is true enough," she told them after her pensive moment. "But it won't stop me from trying to change things. I will not allow the world to make me cynical."

"There's nothing wrong with being cynical," Alan remarked, "if it keeps you grounded to the realistic level."

"When you live on the realistic level," Charlotte said, quietly complementing her husband's point of view, "you may very well change things for the better—at least, once in a while. But don't imagine that the world was made to conform to your will. It doesn't play fair, and it isn't about to change its habits so that you can always win the game." "Complicity with the unexpected is an essential requirement for anyone who wants to meet the world on its own terms," Alan said. "That is the only time when the world will tolerate the bit of wild courage that is in all of us and the romance."

"In spite of the worst of things, there *is* romance," Charlotte said. "There is beauty, too, and favorable adventure, if you know how to see things for what they are."

"That is a lesson I keep learning every day," she said, while she held out her hands and drew them closer to her.

The warm touch of their hands around hers roused the love she felt for them. Apart from that complicated love, she felt a pity, too. Its newness startled her, because her adulation had always received them as perfect and beyond her power to interpret the subtleties of their characters. But with an awakened clarity, she understood now that the war had destroyed something important within them.

Later that day, when dark clouds and an uneasy wind promised a stormy evening, they decided against sailing across the already restless waters in a sturdy yawl which belonged to Alan's friend. Instead, after they returned to the spacious house where they were staying, they gave themselves wholeheartedly to preparing and cooking a fine dinner. Charlotte's fresh herb omelet, Alan's sirloin steaks served with green peppercorns and sautéed potatoes, and Eleanor's cream-puff pastry fritters accompanied by apricot sauce made their meal especially festive. A magnum of *Veuve Clicquot* enhanced their pleasure at the table. On this day, they had been celebrating

Eleanor's having turned eighteen years old a few months earlier. Officially, she was a young woman. This special evening that they were now sharing with her and this special dinner were part of a series of belated birthday celebrations that would continue when Gerald returned from his latest business trip.

So, too, did their conversation, which was as lively as it was varied, enhance their pleasure. They spoke of the achievements of women aviators, including France's Raymonde de Laroche, Germany's Melli Beese, and America's Lilian Gatlin. They remarked upon Paavo Nurmi's recent victories in long-distance running competitions in Finland, his homeland. He was expected to excel in the Summer Olympics, which were to be held in Paris during the following year. An extraordinary athlete from Finland, Nurmi was training to win gold medals for his swift performances in the fifteen-hundred-meter race, in the five-thousand-meter event, in the team cross-country competition, and in the three-thousand-meter race. Alan and Charlotte admired his spending hours upon hours in grueling practice for the games and living on black bread and raw fish.

They also discussed Paul Cézanne's *Monte Sainte Victoire (1904-1906)*. Alan respected its mosaic-like pattern which integrated the land and the sky. The canvas was a monumentality of square brush strokes and sharp edges or planes of color, including cerulean and cobalt blue, viridian green and emerald, cadmium yellow and ochre, and—in the foreground—umber and black. As interpreted by Cézanne, Monte Sainte Victoire was an unconsoling yet majestic solidity. The silhouette of the mountain itself was both a defiant beak and an aggressive prow.

With quiet feeling, Charlotte then spoke of the six songs that Beethoven composed for his sorrow-laden *To the Distant Beloved*. How subtly, Charlotte said, and within a simple, strophic melody, Beethoven conveys throughout the cycle the implicated order that is our memory. Its vivid impress upon our senses calls forth the past within the present, even as it imbues what-once-was with a loss and regret melded with what-is-now and what-will-be-forever. Each of the songs is a landscape which separates. But it is the very first song that invokes the pain of distance. The singer of that melody is a lonely being sitting upon a hill and gazing into a nebulous mist. He is cut off not only from the far-off pastures where in years gone by he had found his beloved, but also from that whole cycle of years which had brought him his best happiness.

As if this talk of Beethoven and the loss of one's best happiness were their inspiration, Alan and Charlotte then spoke of a kayaking adventure which, a few years before the war, they had experienced within the southwestern islands of the Åland Archipelago in Finland. There, on summer recess from their university studies, they paddled along Bronze Age trade routes that connected what is now Russia to Sweden and Northern Germany.

In those days, Alan explained, they rode on the impetus of their bolder venturing. The favor of the world seemed theirs to possess as long as they connected their daring to well-honed skill. It was a tremendous thing to journey with Charlotte five hundred kilometers from a southerly cluster of islands to the southwest coast of the mainland and then east to Helsinki, the capital of Finland. More than a few times, they pitted their determination against abrasive winds and rocky shoals. As they island-hopped among the islets, they kept the crossings short and always looked for shelter.

It felt exotic, Charlotte said, to camp with Alan next to a seal-hunter's hut on Enklinge Island. They also camped in a deserted light tower on Kökar Island and next to a sauna and a church within the harbor of Aspö Village. One time, caught as they were, on the rim and momentum of lashing winds, they and their two guides hauled their boats onto flat rocks, bows pointed in the whirling atmosphere.

"It was positively aboriginal," Charlotte said, "to nestle—there among the jagged rocks—within a rugged crevice which was lined with moss, dried branches, and driftwood."

On those more-than-ordinary days, Alan

reminisced, taking up once more the narrative of their kayaking adventures in Finland, it was splendid to pass gray and red granite cliffs—bedrock rounded by ice glaciers—in the sheer openness of hastening motion. At the edge of the expanding Baltic Sea, they witnessed white-tailed eagles and wily gray herons flying around low, rocky shores that were backed by alder and moss, by stunted pines and dwarfed birch, and by shallow, reed-filled ponds. They passed as fleetly well-worn farm buildings painted with red ochre, and deserted, gray-ancient huts that had once housed fishers and eider hunters.

Splendid as well it felt, whenever they found themselves in the luminous folds of dawn, to tread cautiously across slippery rocks covered with a thin layer of deep-green algae. At noon they read in the clouds the power of the southwest wind, and at night they covered their eyes with scarves and were lulled into peaceful sleep. The brief Nordic nights, filled with light and more light, were themselves a prophecy of the morning sun peering from high above the horizon and a prophecy, too, of warm, comforting air filled with mellifluous bird-song.

In Finland, Charlotte said, they knew together the thrill of confronting effectively the gray-green shoulder-height waves that slapped against their faces as their kayaks, fully loaded, cut heavily through the foaming density of the crests and through roiling gusts of wind. All the while, they soared on motion's swifter hurl. They were pleased then that raw, potent nature had withheld its more fearful dangers and, with no special regard of them, had shared with the elusive moment a show of playful fury.

"One of our guides told us that danger was our friend," Alan said, musing quietly now upon that thought. "Maybe it was."

"Well, danger was definitely playing with us," Charlotte said. "You and I had a good time during that vacation."

"In those years," Alan remarked, with the trace of a wistful smile, "we believed we could make the whole world our friend."

For just an instant, the bright glow of happiness covered their faces. It was a happiness that no other memory had summoned—at least, not while Eleanor was with them. She had listened with special interest to their recollections of summer days which had occurred a decade earlier. The kinetic imagery of their telling reminded her how much she missed kayaking with her school's team. But their looking back to their happiest time reminded her, too, that they carried with them always an unresolved burden of sorrow. She felt such love for them and such pity. Without their quite understanding why she did so, yet cordially accepting her gesture, she rose from her chair and hurried to caress them. Because she was so moved by their muted sadness, she gave each of them a kiss. Her kisses, planted softly upon their lips, brought her a new and thrilling pleasure. Their eyes, misted by the wine they had consumed and by the narratives they had shared with her, gleamed at her touch. The intensity of their glances told her that her kisses had also brought them a new pleasure.

At the close of the evening, Alan and Charlotte persuaded her to recite three poems of which she was especially fond: Elizabeth Barrett Browning's "If thou must love me, let it be for nought / Except for love's sake only"; Emily Dickinson's "I live with him, I see his face"; and Edna St. Vincent Millay's "If in the years to come you should recall."

"I feel very good," Charlotte said, a half-hour later, after they had completed the tasks which returned the dining room and the kitchen to their pristine appearance. "We've brought romance back into our world tonight."

"Let's keep romance for a few hours more, at least," Alan said. He had gathered them to himself and was accompanying them to the master bedroom.

Then, in the next hours when they heard the waves break against the rocks and when the summer rain kept lashing against the French doors that looked upon the balcony and the sea beyond, Eleanor accepted completely this first night of love with them. The light of the lamps upon the tables that flanked the ample bed in which they lay so pleasurably close to each other illuminated Alan's rugged body as he enfolded her within his nakedness, which to her eyes was vivid and persuasive. The light revealed, too, the sensual touch of their fingers and hands as they explored every inch of each other's body. That night she accepted Charlotte's tongue upon her tongue that united them in a long kiss. She also accepted the fragrant kisses with which she touched her forehead and eyes and nose and mouth. But Charlotte's role in this threesome would always be that of a *voyeur*. It was Alan's touch that roused Eleanor especially. Even when he smoothly mounted her and she noticed Charlotte caressing his arched and rugged back, she was pleased that the three of them were there together. Charlotte had placed her body close to her husband's, so that whatever pleasure he took from his new partner would also belong to her. Soon, though, Eleanor forgot that Charlotte was there. The moment that Alan entered her, she collaborated with him alone. For desire was firing their bodies to some adroit and thrilling symmetry.

CHAPTER FOUR

ENTHRALLMENT

In the first days of Alan's erotic influence upon her, Eleanor felt no pangs of guilt. Before the deaths of her parents, her responses to life's alterations had usually been conventional. Her secret yearning for her parents' approval and her quiet pleasure during those times when they recognized the merit of her efforts placed her among the many adolescent girls and young women whose parents often withheld their approval and even their smallest show of affection. Even now, many months after her parents had died, she felt not only lost, but also haunted by their absence. Her lostness derived from her not being able to imagine her life without them. Yet she wanted a life without them. She wanted to discover a way to begin that life, confident and adventurous and original. Confused and uncertain, she had not yet summoned the courage or sighted the episode that would set her free. Her trouble-haunted awareness of her mother and her father kept their influence alive and predominant, even though she was searching for some incident or some person that might help her to escape from them. As formidable and willful after their deaths as they were during their lives, her parents continued to hold her in thrall. Ghostly yet nearly palpable, they went on casting their spells upon her, binding her to their will and refusing to release her from their jurisdiction. Their presence inspired her awe and exhumed the hatred of them that she had always struggled to keep buried.

Only two persons had ever offered her the nurturing care of parents. They were Ann and Keith Sheffield. In that special summer, when she—quietly embittered ten-year-old Eleanor Farrell—felt once more abandoned because her parents chose to be away from her, busy in other countries with their successful careers, Mrs. Sheffield made a surprise entrance into her life as a kindhearted governess who taught her algebra, French, and Latin and so much more. Without fanfare or indoctrination of any kind, she helped her to see the world and herself in new and exciting ways. She brought to their teacher-student relationship hardy youthfulness, athletic prowess, and confident guidance. Tall, raven-haired, and beautiful, she was twenty-six years old and was married to Keith Sheffield, a thirty-five-year-old Newport surgeon whose dark-haired ruggedness and beaming smile made him appear protective and friendly.

It was Mrs. Sheffield, a solid and authentic teacher, and Dr. Sheffield, her equally helpful husband, who understood with awakened clarity the raw powers and unbridled energies of nature. Guided by their instruction, Eleanor came to feel within herself correspondent powers that, gently stirred at first by quickening apprehension, gave her an intense awareness and allowed her to witness the quieter revelations in nature that sometimes awed and surprised her.

In that memorable summer, so essential to her becoming, the Sheffields guided her through the islands of Narragansett Bay—Conanicut, Aquidneck, and Prudence...Dutch, Patience, Rose, and Gould. On those islands, she came to know—while observing the fertile life of tremulous tide pools—the red-brownness of Irish moss seaweed which had washed ashore a day or two and was bleaching already to white. Its flattened blades leaned still away from its short stalk to form firm-grasping fingers with round, blunt tips. She came to know as well, upon sighting it offshore in shallow waters, the yellow bay scallop. The mantle of its shell gleamed with thirty or more blue eyes and its wily alertness propelled it with clapping motion at the Bay's meandering edge, away from an adversarial sea-star or an inquiring girl's nimble hand.

One time she saw a cobalt blue mussel anchored to the sea's white, glittering rock by hardy byssal threads of its own evolving. Later that same season, she watched a black-fingered mud-crab hurrying stout and dark into brackish waters, just before the tooth of its larger claw (a jagged, sun-reflected gleam) crushed the shell of a delicate oyster.

Shortly thereafter, while she was still young in her seeing and earning now at ten years old a reliable independence tethered yet to safe authority, Mrs. Sheffield, and Doctor Sheffield, too, as mentoring substitute parents taught her to swim more adeptly in the coiling July waters of Eastern Beach in Newport. They also taught her to sail across the brisk waves of Conanicut Island, between the Bay's east and west passages. More easterly, they sculled with her on the temperate sheen of Sakonnet River in Little Compton in a boat which Dr. Sheffield and a Scandinavian friend (a fellow surgeon) had built together five years earlier. On that sculling day, she had shared with them—these wonderful substitute parents—a nice precision working in smooth unison the pairs of oars jutting from each side of their vessel. For her part (so Mrs. Sheffield seated behind her noticed), she co-piloted with the boldness of a midshipman or boatswain or quicksilver mariner. Upon arriving with them on the shaded bank of their destination and excited beyond ordinary measure, she was moved to declare an agile girl's genuine enthusiasm.

"This *has* to be my best day of all."

With the parent-like wit to revel privately in her moment and yet assure her of an auspicious future, the Sheffields smiled in agreement.

"Yes, I think it must be your best," Mrs. Sheffield said.

Then she promised her more.

Her motherly composure quietly approved her pupil's merit and, with brown-eyed gentleness, urged her forward to new occasions for a girl's self-mastery.

"There will be other days just as good and some even better."

A few days later at Gould Island, once more in the east passage of the Bay and guided still by the mentoring Sheffields, Eleanor found herself startled—and quite happily—by the purple iridescence of the glossy ibis. A supreme tenaciousness, the ibis waded through the shallows of salt-water marshes and with keener instinct probed the mud with long, insistent bill. Its downward curve smoothly grasped crayfish or crab or moon snail.

It was in this summer, too, that she recognized from a recollected sighting of a previous week which provided her with a first acquaintance, the imperious majesty of the osprey. She sighted it this time at Sachuest Point on Aquidneck Island. Its white head and dark eye-stripe were a different flare upon space and altitude and water. Its three-foot wingspan, deep brown back, and mottled underbody became an enormous power while hovering momentarily over submissive waters just before plunging feet first—a razor-sharp swiftness—to pierce a round blue fish.

Vivid and accurate, nature revealed its beauty and its danger.

During that summer, she enjoyed a camping trip with the Sheffields in the Weetamoo Woods in Tiverton. There, they were in the presence of the East Bay's superior fishing waters, yet at the edge nonetheless of a towering forest of deciduous trees—beech and ash and honey locust. It was within this summery experience that she heard the strong, slurring notes of the tawny ovenbird even before her glance had met in fleet acknowledgement the small bird's incisive eyes-with-bold-white-rings pausing to study her inquiring gait upon the sinuous path of the woods where with accurate confidence she treaded. Sensing no enemy, the wily bird resumed his task of turning over fallen leaves—the better to find a crisp beetle or fat, wriggling worm. It was then, in this specific July, while preparing to launch their skiff on the crystal-bright river which held beneath its waters a multiplicity of fish, that she and the Sheffields saw a white-tail deer leaping with athletic ease into shaded, receding space that was the forest path behind them. Days earlier, she had witnessed the sprint of the snowshoe hare and the scurrying motion of the red squirrel.

It was in that July, though on a warm, sweet-scented night, that she stole away from the sleeping Sheffields and the rough comforts of their camp to experience an adventure all alone.

Launching her skiff with stealthy competence and an already troubled pleasure onto moonlit waters, she—with a rower's accurate agility—pushed her oars against the plash of ripples. She pushed again, propelling her craft with stately evenness away from the rocky cove where, for a night's respite from fishing, she and the Sheffields had decided to camp. Rowing all the while into the luminous space before her, she saw beneath the moon's spectral glow many of the familiar shapes that rendered location a plausible reality: the ferny bank which she was now leaving, the smooth river on which she briskly rode, and vaporous mist rising and wafting a gentle veil or net around her.

Far away in the accurate-seeming distance, on the opposite bank, the still-constant light of the moon revealed silver-tipped bushes and a promising trail. The light offered, as well, the burnished flicker of the trees which on that very day she had walked by or touched or leaned against. Now she saw the gnarled sureties of copper beech, which at noontime had been a fully received imagery of giant, aged trunks and burgundy leaves. In a cool alcove, there rose the beech called by some "weeping," with branches pendulous and with greenness cascading. That tree had made a superior canopy which provided a hiking girl and her caring mentors a comfortable refuge from languorous heat and from a surfeit of exploring.

She saw also the white ascensions of ash trees, stalwart along the secluded path that meandered far away into the woods and invited a young traveler's further reconnoitering. Golden rain trees displayed delicate foliage like bright filigree and fruits lantern-shaped and wafer-like. She could not see them entirely. The kinetic flashes of their forms as well as the expanding linearity of the river and the solidity of the fern-crested banks rose before her seeing as if to maintain her acquaintance with them. But the evening light showed them as swift and merely partial impressions. Her apprehension for that instant was a sleight of eyes seeing in full what was disembodied. Having with palpable satisfaction sighted them completely only hours earlier permitted her now to imagine that the integrity of each of them was there unimpaired in the very place where she had earlier located them. By that means, she felt confidently tethered to the alacrity of her craft and to the reassurance of the space about her and of the sky above.

For the first ten minutes of her secret flight from the camp, all went well. Her sleek pinnace like a stately swan carried her agilely across the river. But then a band of floating clouds began to overtake the stars and the moon. Gradually, the natural forms which to her eyes had, even in the moonlight night, remained familiar were suddenly become alien things, betraying their original imprint upon her perceiving. It was then, while she searched out the opposite bank and sighted at the threshold of the horizon's boundary the summit of the craggy ridge, that her confidence faltered. There, behind the summit of that once-familiar ridge, a dark ambivalence suddenly upreared its head. It was a towering peak with measured motion striding toward her as if in unison with the swift rhythm of her oars. That time, alone on the water, she knew the ghostly hooting of the barred owl and the fearful rustling of the trees in the uncertain distance toward which she was advancing. Or was it they who were advancing toward her? Some far-off dying creature shrieked—a red squirrel perhaps or a hermit thrush being torn into edible pieces by the swift-cutting talons of an owl. Still the looming, ambiguous ridge upreared its head, camouflaged fitfully by the too-casual light of the moon and by the auxiliar glow of temporary stars.

But soon, as if to test her girlhood mettle or trap her inside a cavernous darkness or deliver itself unto the sky's eerie mysteries, the moon disappeared. So too did the stars, leaving her a solitary voyager untethered from the light that joined her to the known. She was without even the fisher's lantern that would have glimmered its definitions of the immediate space before her. In her haste while leaving the camp, she had neglected to bring it into her skiff. Yet, with whatever steel fibers in her heart had not forsaken her, she with consistent oars journeyed onward. All the while she was resisting the thought that the whole of space behind and around and before her—the craggy ridge and towering hills and innumerable trees—were pursuing or closing upon or hurrying toward her.

Only when she had reached the opposite bank did the moon and the stars return, displacing the convoluted gloom of clouds that had, for a time, concealed all luminescence. Then mooring her boat and stepping onto the dew-laden, ferny bank, she stood with cadet stance before the forest of trees observing her. Gathered unto their own darkness, they allowed the glow of new light to touch them with merely oblique appraisal. After turning about to observe in the faraway distance the cragged ridge that watched her with brooding stare and the formidable hills that with imperious calm stood silent, she paused. She felt leagued with them in capable, though somewhat uneasy, fraternity. And that was all of it—this journeying there not as a preface to a night-time exploring of the forest, but as a sign to herself and a notice to the secretive earth that she had consented even in the dark to venture toward whatever mystery was there to meet her.

But a half-hour later, after—in her familiar skiff once more—she had made her way back to the camp, she was grateful nonetheless to find the known reality of the Sheffields sleeping peacefully by the fire's steady light which all the while had stayed with them. Still, she did not—on the following morning or until a week later—tell them of her eerie adventure or of her new distrust, just a little, of pleasant-seeming trees and the solidity of hills and mountains, and the certainty of stars and clouds and moon. Only then, trusting their care of her, would she allow herself to reveal so much of her soul to the matter-of-fact and no-nonsense Sheffields whose good opinion she found indispensable to her well-being.

"Your experience on that night wasn't so different from anyone else's," Mrs. Sheffield told her. "Caught inside that ominous darkness, you felt that nature or some dangerous spirit was holding you in its thrall. You felt as if you were trapped inside some evil enchantment. Sometimes, especially when I was your age, I felt the same way."

"So have I," Doctor Sheffield told her. "Maybe our fear is roused by our anger that something or someone who appears at first to be solacing and protective may become our destroyer."

The Sheffields pleased her with their forthright empathy for what she herself had deemed too sensitive a response to her night on the Weetamoo River—too hesitant or poetic or self-conflicted.

This day, as on so many other days, Doctor Sheffield with wise understatement offered a further remark.

"Almost everyone finds out at one time or another, though not necessarily in a boat traveling through the dark, that the world is an uncertain place. But you have the grit to like it no less and to go on doing your part to make it something better."

Now, eight years later, more frequently than in recent years and right after her parents had died, Eleanor often thought about the Sheffields. She wished that they could come back into her life. At her urging, her grandfather had made inquiries about them through his proficient lawyers. Because of their adept inquiries and to her melancholic dismay, she learned that the Sheffields had remained in England after the war. Doctor and Mrs. Sheffield were devoting themselves to the rebuilding of England. During the war, each of them had served honorably in the American army—he as a dedicated surgeon assigned to battlefields in France and to war-ravaged London and she as his equally dedicated nurse. Now, there in London, they were helping the maimed and the traumatized to reclaim their places in society. With their wealthy friends in America and in England, they were also raising funds that would rebuild the areas where entire neighborhoods in and outside London had been destroyed by the enemy's aerial bombings.

The Sheffields were extraordinary. They were caring and honest and helpful. In these new grieving days, she needed them once again to comfort her. She needed their counsel and their protection. She needed their affection which had never asked more of her than her willingness to keep learning about herself, to help other people, and to maintain a life that was both upright and creative. Without them, she felt utterly lost. Not even the kindness and generosity of her grandfather could appease her longing to be rescued. In his relationship with her, he was often reserved and stiff. He was uncomfortable expressing warmhearted emotions or sharing his personal feelings. Even inside the comforts of his luxurious estate, she felt abandoned. She might have been an outcast on a remote island or a prisoner of her bitterness and her inability to rescue herself.

Then, on a fortunate afternoon in May, when she was beginning to believe that she would never be rescued, Eleanor met Alan and Charlotte Aubray, a different breed of counselors. At the beginning of their friendship, Charlotte was her primary rescuer. She taught her not only advanced mathematics and science, as well as classical literature and several foreign languages. She also convinced her that, in spite of the deaths of her parents, she could reenter the world as an up-to-the-minute young woman who had an aptitude for adventure and for embracing the splendid and sometimes hidden joys of life. In these early weeks of their friendship, Charlotte wove a spell around her and she—forlorn and abandoned Eleanor Farrell— learned to be happy again, at least most of the time. She accepted the gifts of Charlotte's magic. She consented fully to the enthrallment.

Alan was a different sort of spellbinder. He banked his powers. He bided his time. He chose the right moment to bring his magic-seeming emphasis into her conflicted life. He did not in these first weeks move with careless abandon. Nor, at first, did he confuse her senses with prominent displays of his masculine authority and his inherent sensuality. As wily as he was charismatic, he spent a few weeks casting instead his subtle influence upon her. Always, in these weeks, he maintained the courteous language and the charming anecdotes that he directed equally to the other persons in their group as well as to her, if she cared to observe and to listen to him.

Only after he had tested her interest in him as well as his influence upon her did Alan draw closer to her. On several occasions, when he could take time away from his revisionary project for her grandfather's estate, he joined Charlotte and her in their studies of science, mathematics, and languages. Leagued with Charlotte, he made the homeschooling experience for her both productive and enjoyable. He joined Charlotte and her as well in their charitable visits to a children's hospital; a ghetto teeming with poverty, crime, and malnutrition; and a new school for gifted high school students whose parents were hardworking immigrants and recently naturalized citizens.

Eventually, there came days when he spent time alone with her. They went sailing. They played tennis. They swam in her grandfather's pristine swimming pool with its stainless-steel waterfall fountain. They went skydiving and skeet-shooting. They rode palominos on a horse farm that was attached to her grandfather's Newport estate.

Not long afterwards, during nights that became festive and unorthodox, Alan made love to her while Charlotte watched them.

More often now, they made love when Charlotte was not there to observe them. Nor did Charlotte always join them in their various excursions, preferring during some of her free time to offer her nursing skills to a hospital in nearby Middletown.

Then, on a sun-bright morning in June when Charlotte was working in the Middletown hospital and Mrs. Appleton, the housekeeper, was shopping in town for groceries, steaks, and wines, Alan cast a new spell upon Eleanor. He breathed soft words into her ears just before he kissed her.

"I love you," he said. "I love you more than I have loved anyone else. I love you more than life itself."

They were pausing now in their walk along the tawny sands of her grandfather's private beach that fanned outward to the rippling waters of the ocean.

The echoing crash of the waves and the playful gleam of the sun upon the blue-greenwaters granted painterly textures to the scene unfolding around and beyond her. A gray-backed gull was swooping with accurate velocity upon and below the crest of a wind-tossed wave to snatch away a wriggling bluefish. In the distance, a jagged, chalky cliff rose as if preeminent toward white, fluffy clouds and an azure sky. Alone with Alan, with no one else to observe them, she received the nearness of his tall body as a familiar and thrilling sensation. The husky intimacy of his words and the sensual glow of his brown eyes were other sensations that thrilled her.

Eleanor was thrilled once more as he repeated the words that declared his love, making of them a sacred incantation that was part of this ritual of love that he was beginning to celebrate with her.

"I love you so much," he said, his deep voice possessed by heartfelt emotion and erotic need. "I love you more than life itself."

His words pleased her, yet the charm of them roused in her new tensions. She was not ready for so powerful a love. She felt that such a love wanted complete possession of her. So prodigious a love could easily overwhelm her. Alan's words pushed her to answer him with a playful reply. Without abandoning her admiration and her respect for him, she subtly resisted the seriousness of his declaration.

"I love the idea of your loving me, Alan," she said. She was careful to keep the sound of her words both light-hearted and serious. "But you take your loving me too far. Your loving me more than life would, I think, be self-defeating. Love life most of all. Loving life most of all is the best claim for lasting happiness."

Her words did not hold him back. So powerful were his feelings for her that he needed to express once more the truth of them. For a moment there flashed across her mind the revelation that this enchanter was caught inside the spell of his own feelings. The love he felt for her held him in its thrall.

He told her as much.

"Without you, there will be no life for me. Without you, my life will not be worth living."

Despite her unease, Eleanor could not resist the spell that he was casting upon her.

"I do have a loving feeling for you," she said. "You already know that. I've given my body to you many times. I've allowed you in those hours to possess me. But I'm not certain that I want that possession to last a lifetime. I'm just beginning. I love you, but I don't know whether I am in love with you. I don't really know what being *in* love means."

If her words disappointed Alan, he gave no sign of dismay. Instead, he answered her with quiet and comforting intonations.

"Of course, you don't know," he said. "We are just beginning."

"Even beginnings lead to endings," she said. Her soft words carried nevertheless steel-true perceptions. "Besides, you are married to Charlotte. She loves you and needs you."

Alan was quick to answer her.

"Charlotte doesn't really need anybody. She's self-reliant and original. She doesn't need me to make her happy."

Startled and uneasy, Eleanor chose words meant to clarify her feelings about Charlotte.

"Charlotte is my friend," she said. "I don't want to hurt her. She's given her consent to our love affair. Her freewheeling attitude has made me feel very sophisticated and very modern. She told us that our love affair will be good for both of us. But your walking away from your marriage to her is a different matter. It most certainly will hurt her."

"I don't want to hurt her, either. But I don't think I love her in the same way. I'm not certain that I need her. Without that need, Charlotte wouldn't want me. Believe me when I tell you that she wouldn't want to make a mockery of our marriage. She would not want to live a lie. At any rate, I want to find out whether you and I can be happy together."

He moved closer to her and allowed his big athletic hands to take hold of the tips of her delicate fingers. The press of his warm hands upon her fingers disquieted her. Though his touch was gentle, she felt his strength nonetheless. This nearness to him, an altogether pleasing sensation, intensified his presence. Once again, her eyes wakened to the full reality of him—to the heated blood that was rushing through the hands that held her own hand, to the brown eyes that with careful intimacy brought her into his regard of her, and to the full-bodied masculinity that was himself, so suddenly exciting and predominant.

She hurried past these feelings and with words both precise and matter of fact played out this scene that he had willed himself to devise and to initiate.

"Our being together in this way has become too complicated," she said. "I'm not certain that I can handle it. Sleeping with you doesn't violate any of my principles. I believe in loving freely and completely. But I know your wife, and I've made a friend of her. That's the complication. I've had such bad dreams lately. In those dreams, I've seen myself as an uncaring and self-centered woman. I do whatever I want and never count the cost to others. I make people unhappy. I make Charlotte unhappy, even though she tries to hide her unhappiness from me."

Alan found quick words that challenged her

thinking.

"Forget about your dreams," he said. "Throw away your guilt. Stop making Charlotte a martyr. She's tougher than you imagine. She'd laugh at your pity. She'd think you foolish for not wanting to stay in this adventure that we have been experiencing together. I know her well. She would advise us to make use of our time together while we have it. We may never have another chance."

Still, he held the tips of her fingers. Still, he studied her refined loveliness and her well-measured poise. There were in his precise inflections the tinctures of possession as well as yearning. The words that he chose, anchored as they were to the charm and the surprise of who she thought he was, excited her. But she responded cautiously, nonetheless. He intended (she imagined) to keep her consent of him free of self-reproach and regret. Despite the impetus of his words, she lodged a question that situated itself at the cusp of self-reproach and regret.

"Are you really sure that you want to go on with us together, even though you are married?"

Without any hesitation at all, he quickly answered her.

"I'm very sure. Without you, I won't want to go on living. Without you, I won't really exist. I'll be a lost man waiting to die."

She heard in his voice a raw excitement and a hint of despair that his clipped words and his husky timbres could not conceal. Again, her unease rose up as if it would overtake her. There was a fear in her that, once she consented to be with him for all the time that her fate would grant her, Alan would take control of her life. She detected in his manner an intensity not unlike the kind of romantic obsession that, eventually, might overtake his mind and spirit, his body and soul. He wanted that same obsession to overtake her, as well. Though he was far more experienced than she in the ways of love, she was not going to succumb to the dangerous currents of his desire and to all the sly efforts he made to enthrall her, to hold her spellbound within his purposes. She would not permit him to appropriate her freedom. On this bright summer day in her young time, she was determined to maintain her independence and to savor whatever pleasures she might experience from their love affair.

CHAPTER FIVE
NEARLY RECKLESS ABANDON

The hardened part of Eleanor's nature, still testing its powers, resisted the groundswell of Alan's obsession and the seismic disturbance of his will upon her plans for her life and upon the decisions that would turn those plans into an adventurous reality. Without even a pause now she held herself steady. She was determined to go forward with the scenario that she envisioned for her own life. Alan might not play a part in that scenario. Possibly, he would, but only on her terms, with her freedom intact and with a proper respect for her freedom. She was not going to allow him or any other man to dominate her. The love affairs she inhabited would have to be collaborations of desire, even though her plan altered in a radical way the steps that Alan had already devised for the two of them together. Made uneasy because of his all-or-nothing approach to their relationship, she took the step that she regarded as most necessary.

"I am very sure that I want to be with you," she said, in that same hour when he declared his undying love for her. "But I have one condition. You must not steal away my freedom. You must leave me room to experience the world as an individual, free and inquiring and original. I do not plan to be an appendage to your will or to any other man's."

She was negotiating with him—her freedom in exchange for the coupling of their fervid bodies and their erotic desires. She was also gambling. The openness of her negotiation might dismay him and might compel him to believe that she had far more experience of men than she led him to believe. That she had brought to him her virginal body, that she had resisted the blunt overtures of youths her own age, should be counted as a special value in whatever transactions she and Alan made in their love affair. Her resistance to his plan for them, her hesitation because of his proprietary manner, might fire his displeasure. But she was counting on the impassioned and reckless love he felt for her. She was beginning to understand that love like his gave no quarter to hesitation or dismay or distrust. In time, if they went their separate ways, he might look back and regard her as a casual mistress. That aspersion would depreciate her value. For Alan, it might make their breakup tolerable. But she hoped that he would tell himself afterwards, after their days and nights together were finished, that she was an extremely clever woman.

Her unflinching awareness of the woman she was

now and of the woman she intended to become pushed her forward into the journey that she had already begun. She wanted to be strong-willed, fearless, and perceptive. She wanted to be *that* Eleanor—a young woman resisting a societal order in which all women faced formidable obstacles in their quest for autonomy. Her parents, too ambitious on her behalf and too ruthless, had taken their places among those formidable obstacles. With his conservative ways, her grandfather might become another obstacle. She had to become a woman with a heart made of steel fibers. The lessons that she learned from her parents—lessons that they may not have realized they were imparting to her—taught her that she must be a little ruthless even in her most personal relationships. Unwittingly, perhaps, their responses to friends who were entangled by unhappy marriages and illicit affairs taught her other lessons, as well. In their male-dominated society and in a time of unquestioned inequities within the relations between men and women, the price that love exacted was often too large to warrant even a bit of happiness. She must find a man who wanted to collaborate with her rather than appropriate her freedom. Whether Alan could become that man, she was not certain.

Her uncertainty brought to their affair both mystery and tension. The unknown elements within their relationship intrigued her. If she was playing with fire, the vivid glow teased her senses and drew her closer to its flames.

Right after she remarked that she did not want anybody to steal away her freedom, Alan—with quiet words and unflinching purpose—reassured her that he did not plan to become a love thief.

"Believe me when I tell you that I don't want to steal anything from you. I want to give. I want to give you everything that I am and that I have."

His quiet words soothed her spirit and sent her suspicion scattering. His words brought a smile to her lips. "Well, kind sir, I believe that you and I can continue to have a happy time together. We are about to begin a new episode. Let's make it work. Let's make it memorable."

"I'm all for that," he said as a smile touched his lips as well. "I like new episodes. I enjoy the unknown. I always find adventure in it."

So, they went forward to days and days of new contentment and the spontaneous arrival of different kinds of happiness. But not every day brought her happiness. There still persisted her anguished feelings about her parents and their contempt for whatever weakness her schoolgirl fears and hesitations exposed. Even after their deaths, she raged against their mistreatment of her. Yet, despite their austere demands of her and their coldhearted ambitions for her, she required their living presence. They had been her ballast against confusion. They were her legal protectors who made her feel safe even though her leaderly achievements at school never satisfied them. In their coldhearted ways, they had abandoned her even while they lived. But they were alive then. They would, she believed, come to her rescue if she were imperiled in any way. Now, they were no longer alive. They were dead, and in their vanishment she felt vulnerable and inadequate. In those moments when, bitter and regretful, she felt utterly abandoned, her fear and depression left her trembling and weeping.

Now there was new ballast in her life. There were grandfather and Alan and Charlotte. There was, best of all, prodigious and extraordinary and wily Alan.

She did understand how much this Newport summer was changing things for her. She did perceive that her ambivalent feelings for Alan were the stirrings of love made uneasy and imprisoning.

In the weeks that had so swiftly passed, Alan had avoided being alone with her. Now, in late June, during his free time from his revision of her grandfather's property and with Charlotte's jaded consent and equally jaded testing of her marriage to Alan, he arranged private meetings and occasional excursions with her. They water-skied across the waters of Narragansett Bay, forty miles away from her grandfather's Newport estate. They went skydiving from an airfield in Boston.

They rode palominos on her grandfather's horse farm a mile away from his home and still a part of his estate. They made love in one of the secluded cottages on his estate. They dined in a luxurious beach hotel in Greenwich, Connecticut. During their days alone together, without her uncle or his devoted staff hovering about them, Alan became before her pensive eyes someone else, someone different from the hard- driving and ambitious engineer that she had taken to be his accurate personhood. Dressed in an ivory linen suit or a royal blue jacket paired with beige trousers rather than in blue denim coveralls, he looked even more ruggedly handsome. No longer constrained by his too- intense work ethic, he was free to inhabit the persona of a young, cosmopolitan gentleman. It was a role, she thought, that suited him admirably. There was in him at times a debonair manner, a witty engagement with the world, and a muted sensuality that suggested the bright fires he had discreetly banked.

Wary at first of her new, more thrilling impression of him, she studied Alan with a gaze as careful as it was congenial. On one occasion, she took special note of his cool assurance when a formidable Swiss banker confronted the both of them at the dining table they were occupying for that afternoon as husband and wife at the hotel in Greenwich. The table came with a beachfront view of colorful sailboats hurrying across the excited waves of the blue-green sea, the sight and sound of gray gulls soaring toward fluffy clouds, and the swift energies of young couples swimming with carefree exuberance.

"The hotel has always assigned this table to me," the banker said. "The *maître d'* made a mistake. This table belong to me."

The banker was a middle-aged man, apparently used to having the people around him fulfill his every need. She had met his type before. Tall, silver-haired, and burly, his Wall Street success did not soften the rough character of his face or his arrogance.

Alan eyed him directly. If he disliked this man, he made no outward show of his feelings. To the banker's demand that he give him the table, Alan responded through words that tempered their cutting edge with a natural buoyancy.

"You are traveling alone," he said. "But this table needs the company of a good woman. Bring your wife next time, and the table may very well belong to you."

The banker was fuming.

"Don't take it so hard, old sport," Alan told him. "Sit down and have a drink."

Grim-faced and disapproving, the banker turned away without replying.

Together, both of them watched the *maître d'*

(apologetic and meticulous) guide the banker into a dining room nearby.

"Too bad," Alan said to her. "He could have enjoyed this table for at least a quarter of an hour."

She liked Alan's irony and his self-control.

There were other occasions when she noticed Alan's quick-witted reactions and his generous nature.

One afternoon, while they were having lunch in a Nantucket hotel dining room, a nervous young waiter brushed against a glass of water that spilled upon Alan's hands. Not a whit annoyed by the accident, he quickly put the waiter at ease.

"Well," he said, "that's one way to clean my hands."

More than once, she noticed the sense of humor he brought to any scattershot mishap (swinging his golf club too hard and too fast and failing to strike the ball in the middle of the clubface) or to an unexpected complication (a wrong turn on a rain-swept country road). He knew how to laugh at his fate and still keep it as an ally. This ingrained self-control increased the respect that she had always accorded him.

For many days afterwards, Eleanor recalled these occasions. But not until several days after they occurred was she willing to admit that, in each of these incidents and with extemporaneous and accurate responses, Alan had revealed something important about himself. She was learning to admire his good-natured humor and his sense of fair play. She was learning as well to like his generous spirit and the courtly manner in which he escorted her to a dining table or to a waiting car or into a country club where he so easily drew her with him into the general merriment. Now she accepted the warmth of his hand upon her own as they sauntered across a hotel's afternoon courtyard to peer at the sun-touched mountains that gleamed like phosphorescent bodies. She accepted as easily the touch of his face against her own as his body leaned into hers while they were sauntering along the tawny sands of a beach. She welcomed his nearness when they were swimming and whenever they approached the swerve of an intricate wave. Always before, whenever she had seen him in her uncle's home, Alan had been a strong physical presence. Here, during these daytime excursions to Martha's Vineyard, Nantucket, and Cape Cod, he was even more vivid. Suddenly, because she was not really anticipating her new sight of him, she perceived him as a worthy lover.

What impressed her most of all was the sensual hold that he was beginning to have upon her. She enjoyed being with him. At a hotel within Martha's Vineyard where they stayed as man and wife, they swam in the blue-green waters of the heated pool as if they were long-time partners who had perfected their synchronous movements. One time, while they were cavorting in the water, she happened to touch the smooth skin of his chest.

The touch, which was more like a caress and lasted only a moment, excited her. If she closed her eyes, she might have believed that she was touching him while they were in bed together. This time the thought did not disconcert her. Rather, it persuaded her that in many ways Alan was proving to her that she had a profound need of him.

Her bond with him deepened. One happy weekend allowed them to spend more time together as a romantic couple in her grandfather's home. Her grandfather and Sylvia, his discreet and cosmopolitan friend, were visiting friends on Saranac Lake in upstate New York, and Charlotte was spending a few days in Camden, Maine, visiting an aged aunt who had for many years made an impressive career as a novelist. During this happy weekend, Alan and Eleanor sailed in mid-afternoon across the lake behind her grandfather's home. Always compatible and always collaborating in this new partnership between them, they dined at a country club in Newport on salmon in Champagne sauce and danced in the later hours of that same evening. Through all of their hours together, she felt her spirit reaching out to him. He, in turn, reveled in the sheer wonder of being alive with her beside him.

"You've given me new life," he said. "I feel reborn. And yet I feel the same—not as I have been in these war years, but as I used to be when I was a student who thought he could make a very happy life rebuilding large country estates and luxurious penthouses in big cities."

The tremendous change that was taking hold of her gave her new eyes. She was perceiving Alan in new ways. How human he was. How extraordinary. How self-contained and magnificent. It lifted her spirits to watch his masculine assurance and to listen to his clear- sighted remarks about music, painting, architecture, and aviation. Nor did he require that she merely listen. Eagerly, he sought out her view of things. Together, they collaborated within dialogues that were as crisp as they were original.

That they were well-trained pianists who often played classical music made her feel even closer to him. One of their conversations about music drew from each of them comments about the emotional intensities of Claudio Monteverdi's opera *The Return of Ulysses*. Both she and Alan admired this opera about Ulysses because it centered on an individual who, having fought his way through ten years of war, went on to surmount tremendous obstacles when he returned to find that corrupt men had overtaken his homeland. In Monteverdi's portrayal of him, influenced as it was by Homer's epic poem, Ulysses was an extraordinary man who identified himself bravely to a hostile universe.

"Monteverdi is the Italian Homer, and Shakespeare, too" Alan said, "because of his understanding of human nature."

"Yes," she agreed. "Monteverdi makes us understand that there are no certainties even for wily and heroic men like Ulysses. The world is filled with violence and betrayal and unbearable sadness."

One afternoon, she and Alan visited an exhibit of the Symbolist prints of Edvard Munch. He was a Norwegian artist, whose last name was pronounced as Moonk and who was famous because of his portrayals of the conflicted relationships between men and women. Until the war came, Munch had often visited Alan's father, whom he regarded as a loyal friend and an eminent collector of American, European, Asian, and African art. They had first met many years earlier when his father attended an exhibit of Munch's art in Oslo, Norway. With his father and sometimes with him, Munch shared lively conversations whenever he stayed with them for a few days in their villa at Saint-Jean-Cap-Ferrat on the French Riviera. He was a white-haired rangy gentleman whose presence dominated a room. His brown eyes glowed behind wire-rimmed glasses, their quickened gaze drawing into their awareness the persons and the objects before him. Even then, when he was in his seventies, his sculptured demeanor retained a worn handsomeness. But his large, strong hands were his most memorable feature. They were hands that were inspired by a first-rate mind. During his long career, they had created thousands of prints, paintings, watercolors, and drawings, as well as hundreds of copper plates, lithographic stones, and woodblocks.

Alan remembered fondly Munch's discussions with him and his father about his Symbolist art. For him, the very elements of the material world such as a tree, the sky, a bed, or a face were signs or correspondences of underlying moods, emotions, and ideas.

Eleanor had never met Edvard Munch. But she had studied his art when she was a student in Farmington, Connecticut.

Here in Newport, one print in particular drew her special praise. It was called *Consolation*. Munch had composed its imagery in drypoint and aquatint, which he then printed in black on Japan paper. The narrative it suggested involved a nude man embracing a nude woman on the edge of a bed. The woman is weeping. Perhaps, the man is leaving her, or she is remorseful after having given in to passion.

As she studied the print in the company of Alan, Eleanor became uneasy. Against her conscious will, she was sexually aroused as she looked at the naked couple that Munch had brought to life in his print. Yet it was not the print alone that aroused her. It was the presence of Alan and the influence of his body next to hers, there within the impressive Newport Museum. Standing close to her as they studied Munch's art, Alan's long body pressed against her own, and his brown-eyed handsome face touched her cheeks as though he intended to kiss her.

She thought of her resolution to maintain her independence from Alan. She tried to push away her guilt so that she could savor this special time with him.

To displace her unease, she began commenting upon Munch's print. She used her remarks to remind Alan of her plan to remain self-determining even though she had entered an intensely romantic relationship with him.

"If I hadn't studied Edvard Munch's art at school and enjoyed many scholarly lectures about his work," she said, "I might be surprised that he is so honest about the role of the woman in a love affair. Few men, I think, admit the truth of their relations with women. In this print, Munch exposes the vulnerability of the woman. It is she who loses most in a love affair. She is the one who compromises herself and risks being punished by society."

Again, she thought of Alan. The intensity of his love pleased her. But his love for her, which was becoming an obsession, was problematic. Her knowledge of him, drawn from their brief time together, convinced her that he wanted his life completely intertwined with hers. Her body and mind and spirit were private territories that he had claimed for himself. She saw his proprietary hold upon her as a sign of his insecurity. He feared losing her. That fear was a weakness that stirred her ambivalent love of him and her pity.

Alan took gentle hold of her hands now. He was, she felt, thinking about her words that told him how much women lose in their relationships with men. If he detected the bitterness in those words, he gave no evidence.

"It won't be that way with us," he said. "That is a promise."

"I am pleased to hear that," she said. "That makes you different from most men."

For a moment, he held her in his gaze. Her words did not influence him to smile, perhaps (she felt) because he regarded those words as an essential part of the love that was growing between them. Instead, he raised her hands to his lips and kissed them.

The gesture filled her with awe. There was so much love in this man, and he was drawing her into its powers.

Now he proceeded to say what he thought about Munch's print.

"I like its indeterminacy," he said. "I also admire the artist's subtle use of shadow to portray an environment that is as ambivalent as it is sensual. We don't know why the woman is weeping or whether her relationship with the man is ending or beginning."

"Not even the man or the woman may know that," she said. "That is part of their mystery."

Now Alan did smile.

"For a young woman who has spent most of her life apart from any suitor," he said, "you know some of the important things about men and women."

"Sometimes I know," she said. "Most of the time, I make my way through the dark, as do many people."

She was moving through the dark right now, and with ingrained wiliness she was keeping her fear at bay.

One Saturday afternoon, after they had spent an hour riding bay-and-white Tobianos on her grand-father's horse farm, they spoke of aviation. They were standing by the split-rail fence enclosing the paddock, where their Tobianos and five or six other breeds, including Arabians and Appaloosas, were grazing. That she had learned to fly a plane pleased him immensely. Because of her grandfather's influence, she had been a pupil of the renowned racing pilot Michel Detroyat. That year, she was only fifteen. After Alan listened to her experience of flying a Mauboussin M.200, he praised her adventurousness and her skill. She perceived in his words a genuine empathy for all that she had been telling him.

"You must be very good," he said. "Detroyat works only with pilots who demonstrate an exceptional skill."

"I think that he took pity on me. I wanted so much to be a good flyer. But at that time I was so awkward and uncertain."

"Oh, I imagine that he saw more than that. He saw your adventurousness and your courage."

Alan's praise moved her. Her grandfather had often praised her flying, but in an understated manner. Whatever proficiencies she achieved as a pilot, he took for granted. After all, many other women (though, perhaps, not so young as she) had proved their courage during the recent war as brave pilots in the Women's Air Transport Auxiliary. Those women were an important part of the Allies' war team. She wasn't, her grandfather reminded her, doing anything that other female pilots had not already done. There was in his attitude, she felt, a genuine respect for her work. He did not want to single her out for special praise that might eclipse the achievements of those war- time women. To do so would be to treat her as if she were an amateur who needed en-couragement.

She liked her grandfather's attitude. Never did he condescend to her. Always, he treated her as a granddaughter who must try to attain the highest standards in all of her efforts.

Yet she saw in Alan's praise of her an empathy that her grandfather sometimes lacked. Though he had known her for only a few months, Alan was more sensitive to her need for praise. He was also more willing to share with her the plans that would make his life after the war both creative and useful. His future involved his drawing upon his knowledge not only of civil and mechanical engineering, but also his knowledge as an aeronautical engineer. He had earned degrees in these various levels of engineering.

It pleased him to tell her of his dream of designing a new plane that might be a more advanced brother to the Siebel Si.202 Hummel.

"As a sports plane, the Hummel has proved itself to be very effective," he explained. "It is a small low-wing cantilever monoplane equipped with side-by-side seating for two and designed to accept a variety of single engines of nine cylinders or so. At its best, the Hummel can attain a speed of ninety-six miles per hour. But the sports plane that I am designing will be made of metal rather than wood. It will have a larger wingspan, and it will be powered by a jet engine."

Once again, Alan's knowledge and enthusiasm impressed her. Once more, Eleanor imagined that he must have been a very fine man before the war, when he was very young and could enter the world on his own terms and with unstinted hope. Even as he believed that he was becoming someone new in her presence, so also did she tell herself that she was turning into someone else. No longer was she always the inhibited young woman with whom she had made a well-examined acquaintance. That woman often belonged to her past. With Alan, she was on those uninhibited days someone not herself—a stranger free to be drawn into nearly reckless abandon and intimacy that lived at the cusp of danger.

Toward this intimacy on those days when she felt

inhibited, she moved with a tension that Alan mistook for her lack of experience. He did not mind when, on their first afternoon away from her bedroom in her grandfather's home and at the moment that he began undressing, she seemed to withdraw from the agreement she had made with him. He was about to make love with her in the bedroom of the secluded cottage on her grandfather's estate.

The unfamiliar room made her suddenly apprehensive.

"I'm not ready for this," she told him while her voice became a tremulous whisper. "This room… this cottage…make everything different. I need more time."

"I understand," he said. "Don't worry about it."

But she was worried, not only about the room, but also about their relationship. She wondered whether she had gone too far. Alan was a married man, and his wife was her friend. More than a few times, he had asked her to make love with him in the secluded afternoon cottage on grandfather's estate, rather than in her nighttime bedroom. Alone together and away from grandfather's staff and unexpected visitors, they could revel in daytime lovemaking. So urgent did Alan's need of her become, that she wondered whether he would force himself upon her once she slipped into bed beside him. Or, possibly, his manly presence would rouse her and, with no inhibitions to hold her senses taut, she would open herself to receive him.

She need not have worried.

That first afternoon together in the secluded cottage, Alan did not make love to her. Instead, he lay beside her — his dark-haired, bronzed handsomeness and naked body caught in the glow of the sun that illumined their bed and lingered by it, as if watching them. His brown eyes gleamed as well, and his penis hung distended. Still, he would not touch her. She saw that he wanted her to become more at ease with his rugged body beside her. He wanted her to recognize the care and love and respect that he had for her. At the same time, he was testing his own capacity for self-willed disciplines. Though he was eager to make love to her, she realized that he would on this afternoon enjoy the game of celibacy that her returning inhibitions required of him. For a half hour and more, while they softly spoke of the travel they might experience together if ever they were married and of the homes they could share in London, Paris, and Buenos Aires, he studied the lovely curve of her figure, her firm breasts, and her light-brown pubic hair. Her beauty, her soft skin, and her fragrance roused his desire for her. But he would not touch her. Then, because he had passed whatever test he had devised for himself and because he had given her a chance to lie next to him while studying him in his nakedness, he turned away from her and fell into a solacing afternoon sleep.

A new dismay lived in her now. Lying next to his nakedness and observing all the details of Alan's well-endowed muscularity *had* aroused her. The affection that she had suppressed during this secret visit to the secluded cottage now flared up before her conscious awareness. Guilt overtook her, and the fear that she was betraying Charlotte and herself stung at her pride and her self-respect. It was this guilt that gave her pause, struggling with her to hold her excited senses still. But her guilt, tentative and confused, was not strong enough to alter her feelings. She was relieved that the afternoon had not destroyed her love affair with Alan. Yet she was also disappointed that Alan had not made love with her. The desire that had taken hold of her was urging her with raw and familiar intensities to bring him, naked and erect, inside her.

Whenever they met thereafter, though, Alan did make love with her. Everything between them seemed new and extraordinary. Even the simple act of squeezing the end of a condom between her forefinger and thumb and placing it over his erect penis thrilled her. He had cast a spell over her. She was a woman made new by the ecstasy of their lovemaking. Vigorous yet gentle, he drew her willingly into that ecstasy.

"You know more than I thought you would," Alan said, as they lay back against the ample and comforting pillows of their bed after the second week of making love.

He felt, she could see, as sated and renewed as she was. That she appeared to be a more experienced lover than he was anticipating did not disturb him. His manly self-possession persuaded him, she imagined, to attribute herease and her versatility to his prowess as a lover. The clue that her careful words now threw out to him was, she felt, just as convincing an explanation.

"Why should my knowing how to behave with a man in a bedroom surprise you?" she began. "I have a wonderful aunt, after all—my father's sister. She is a modern woman. She is artistic. She is educated. She is genteel. She loves her husband very much. She told me what I needed to know. She once said that, if I wanted to keep my husband happy, I must leave modesty outside the door to the bedroom."

Her explanation, which she imparted with precise and cool-headed intonations, drew from him none of his own words. But he studied her with new interest, all the while offering her an enigmatic smile.

By the third week of their lovemaking, she was responding with furious sensuality to his every move. He was an accomplished lover who played upon her body as though it were a musical instrument. Now she gave herself freely to him. Neither her troubled awareness of what she was doing nor the self-loathing that haunted her in solitary hours afterwards held her back. She longed for his touch, whether it was vigorous or gentle.

She yearned for the spermatic scent that was a part of his nakedness. She craved the erotic gestures through which he brought her to multiple and extended orgasms.

By the final days of their time in Newport, she felt that her body and Alan's completed each other. When they made love, no matter the sensual techniques they used to fire their blood, their bodies were in perfect coital alignment. A vigorous lover, Alan made her feel complete and whole—in and away from their bed. She accepted Alan as an ideal partner. In so many important ways—in their intellect, in their courage, and in their sexual prowess—they were similar. In their sensual relationship, they might have been embodied spirits whose every consummation the kinder Fates had ordained. So, she willed herself to imagine, finding in that thought a temporizing judgment—a verdict that appeased her guilt and excused her aberration. Now she began to tell herself that she could be happy only if Alan remained in her life.

At the moment, Alan was very much a part of her life. So intense was her desire for him in these Newport days she was sharing with him, that she brought a nearly reckless abandon to their lovemaking. Each time he mounted her, in the morning or in early afternoon or sometimes at night, she consented to him completely. Always, she consented to the push and thrust and swell of his rhythms, firing as they did her need and her eagerness to collaborate with him to achieve a nearly perfect symmetry.

Rarely, in the rapturous days of being with Alan in Newport or Nantucket or Martha's Vineyard, did she think about Charlotte. Not even during her most excited meeting with Alan when, just before they made love, Alan slipped a diamond ring on the third finger of her left hand and whispered, "We're married," did she think of Charlotte. Only during a weekend in July, after Alan and Charlotte were visiting a young married couple in Saranac Lake within upstate New York did she think about Alan's wife. Once more, while she in that same weekend was visiting her aged aunt, the renowned novelist, in Camden, Maine, her guilt rose up to accuse her, leaving her as unhappy as she was uncertain about her future. She had a loving feeling for Alan and would have gladly lived with him, unmarried. But that was not possible. Besides, her keen-eyed sense of their relationship reminded her that, one day, he might betray her just as he was betraying Charlotte. Her matter-of-fact understanding of things made her see clearly where she stood with Alan and Charlotte and with her society. From her clear-eyed perspective, her continuing her love affair with Alan could only bring the three of them to grief.

There were other problems.

Alan wanted to marry her. But, as much as she had

a loving feeling for him, body and soul, as much as his charismatic presence enthralled her and influenced her to give herself to him with nearly reckless abandon, she did not want to marry him. She needed to discover some fortunate chance that could free her from him and save them all.

CHAPTER SIX
COMPLICATED LOVES

Suddenly, without even a vague intimation or an abrupt warning of any kind, surprise caught hold of Charlotte. It seized her, as though it were a snare or noose entangling her senses, making of her a trapped and injured bird. No memory of her passionate nights alone with Alan or of their days and days of splendid adventuring prepared her for the disquiet that entangled her certainty and with slipknot proficiency bound her inside its prison. Surprise, adamant and punishing for three anguished days and nights, made her at first helpless and confused. Then, roused by anger to the privacy of new awareness and to the impetus of self-determination, she broke free of surprise. Truth, rugged and austere and absolute, came forth from the shadows where she had so carelessly abandoned it. Once again, as advocate and protector, Truth guided her to a full comprehension of the harsh reality of her situation.

Alan had fallen in love with Eleanor.

Whether it was the delicacy of Eleanor's younger beauty that drew him to her, or his awakening her to the fiercest pitch of sexual ecstasy, or her need for Alan's vigorous thrusting and stroking inside her very young vagina, Charlotte did not care to guess. What she did perceive with the clarity of realistic appraisal was the sheer joy that Alan and Eleanor experienced whenever they were together. Her keen-eyed discovery of their excited alliance left her shaken and dismayed. Alan's falling in love with Eleanor and Eleanor's falling in love with Alan were not part of the rebellious and subversive scenario to which, in wifely partnership with Alan two months ago, she had consented. Their mutual enjoyment of Eleanor as an enthralled member of their unorthodox threesome was meant as a capricious escapade. With blind luck or wild chance, their sensual partnership might offer them, Alan and her, temporary solace from the blighted lives that they were condemned to live after witnessing, close up and face-to-face, the savagery and futility of the recent war.

The ghastly memories and ghostly apparitions of that war still burned, furtive and insistent, within the darkest corners of their minds. Alan seldom talked about the booming sounds of the howitzer cannons hurling their deadly projectiles or the wailing of high, far-traveling shrapnel shells or the rapid rattle of stuttering rifles or, closer than that, the sound and sight of dark blood gargling and spilling from a pale recruit's lungs corrupted by poison gas. Only once, after bolting out of a nightmare and crying out his anguish and after allowing her in their amply cushioned bed to comfort him, did he speak of the incessant and shattering bombardments, the exploding trenches and bunkers, the bodies of boyish men engulfed by flames, and the sight and stench of rotting corpses strewn across acres and acres of battlefields. She, too, rarely mentioned what her war-time experiences as a nurse had shown her: the maimed bodies and broken spirit of the brave youths whom the war kept alive even after it had destroyed them.

Rather than talk about this horrific past except in rare, unexpected moments, she and Alan had hurried forward to a new and busy life here in Newport, Rhode Island. With anticipation that sometimes felt like exhilaration, they often improvised scenarios for their post-war existence. Here, on Gerald Marnham's palatial estate, they took pleasure in upending his conservative strictures, especially when he was absent because of business dealings with millionaire executives or because of social occasions with friends of long standing—all of these meetings taking place on the West Coast or in New York, Chicago, Pittsburgh, London, Paris, Rome, Hong Kong, and Johannesburg. Subtle and persuasive, Alan and she were gambling with the Fates that set the rules for right-minded living and that were not opposed to considering the merit of unorthodox choices. Until now, Alan and she had been winning the game.

Lately, though, Alan had been revising the game. With

casual indifference to her feelings, he often excluded her in his meetings with Eleanor. One time at dawn, when golden hues and a roseate blush filled the darkened blueness of the sky and scattered across the wind-quickened waves of the ocean, she saw them—Alan and Eleanor—sauntering hand in hand along the tawny sands of the beach. Eleanor was wearing a white dress and white sandals. Alan's navy polo shirt, white trousers, and navy boat shoes enhanced his casual masculinity. This first time that she caught sight of them, bonded romantically without her, she had wakened from an unhappy dream that had left her forlorn and alone. The dream preceded the here-and-now reality of their betrayal and their tryst.

Hers was a dream of the passionate love that she and Alan shared—an authentic love long cherished and suddenly lost. While she was caught inside that trouble-haunted dream and while she was held prisoner of its sinister implications, she kept reaching out to Alan. Before he pulled away from her, they had been walking together in the dream along a trail that was drawing them into the greenery of a forest. Yellow birch, white spruce, and black ash trees stood tall and proprietary like sentries that were lining the circuitous and mysterious trail. The excited sounds of tree birds filled the air: the high-pitched nasal calls of blue-gray gnatcatchers, the trembling bleats of white-breasted nuthatches, and the chirruping phrases of scarlet tanagers. In the same instant, a tawny-colored rabbit scurried across the path that Alan and she were treading. A red fox with black markings on his feet and ears and a white tip on his tail followed in swift pursuit. Though at this time Alan looked back at her and, with a frown, recognized who she was, he quickly turned away. He hurried forward to join Eleanor, who touched his lips with a delicate kiss and clasped his rugged hand as they journeyed away from her. She kept running toward them, but she could never reach them. An eerie glow overtook their flight from her. In that very moment, they disappeared inside the forest's great wall of darkness.

Still she ran toward the place where they had vanished. This time, her tremulous voice called out a plea—not to Eleanor, but to Alan alone.

"Don't leave me, Alan! Don't leave me!"

Only an echo of her voice answered. Her soul-fed words rose and fell away, plaintive and unanswered by Alan. Her intuition or, perhaps, her keen-minded understanding of her situation, told her that Alan and Eleanor had hastened out of the forest.

Abandoned and dismayed in her dream, she turned away and made her way out of the forest, leaving behind the ghostly trees that stood like soldierly apparitions and leaving behind as well the chattering birds and the wily fox and the scurrying rabbit. As soon as she emerged from the foreboding darkness of the forest, the radiance of a new day rose before her. With quickened steps and returning hope, she made her way toward the beach. Her memory of all the wonderful times that she and Alan spent there together persuaded her that Alan—and, yes, Eleanor too—might be waiting for her there.

But no sooner did she arrive at the beach, than her startled eyes apprehended the truth. Alan and Eleanor *were* there, blanketed on the tawny sands of the private beach. But they were not waiting for her. Held to the privacy of the beach, heedless of any trespasser and of the restless waves that were rushing toward the shore, Eleanor had entwined her long, supple legs around Alan's waist and had raised her hips to meet his thrusts. Her eyes were half-closed, and a smile was touching her mouth because of the pleasure he was giving her. She began moaning because of the depth and pace of his thrusts. In this very moment that she—the wife that he had abandoned—caught sight of him, Alan's eyes were glowing with love for Eleanor. His mouth was partly open. He had reached the peak of excitement, and he was nearly breathless. A raw cry of pleasure and an equally erotic groaning escaped from him. With vigorous thrusting, he was shooting his sperm deep inside Eleanor's vagina. Climaxing at the same time, giving herself completely to their mutual ecstasy, Eleanor moaned with satisfaction.

In that very instant, she—Charlotte Dussolier Aubray,

bonded in an odd yet adventurous marriage with Alan Aubray, who was an extraordinary man that she truly loved—leaped up, cried out her protest at his betrayal, and escaped her dream.

Leaning against a galaxy of pillows, she turned for reassurance to Alan, whom she expected to find sleeping next to her.

"Alan," she called to him, "Alan. Wake up, please. I need to hear your voice. I need you to hold me in your arms. I have had such a terrible dream."

Dawn light was only partially revealing the white pillows and flat sheets and navy blankets that usually brought comfort to Alan as he slept. She expected to see his handsome profile and a portion of his rugged nakedness. What she saw instead were pillows and sheets that held as an intimate possession the vague press of Alan's body before he had tossed the blankets aside and hurried away from his place in the bed as well as from her sleeping form. Startled into a new and ominous awareness and caught inside a tighter breathing, she hurried from the bed and went in search of Alan. That she was wearing her full-length sapphire blue silk nightgown and matching robe eased her apprehension. Alan had once told her that she wore the nightgown and the robe with the authority of a princess.

Minutes later, apprehension returned, a wily presence that some adversarial Fate sent there to observe her. Alan was not in his study, which was located on the second floor of the main house, next to their bedroom in the south wing. There, he sometimes spent the hours right after dawn to review his plan for the suspension bridge that he and his proficient crew were building over a stream that bisected the north area of the Marnham estate. Nor was he seated at the polished mahogany table in the pristine kitchen on the first floor of the south wing, where he usually drank his morning coffee while glancing through the previous day's business mail.

Was he with Eleanor?

Moving swiftly with cautious paces as if she were some Spirit sent here to observe the wayward inhabitants of the Marnham estate, she hurried down a long, wide corridor to the east wing of the main house. When she arrived at the door to Eleanor's bedroom, she neither paused before it nor knocked upon it. Without any hesitation at all, she opened the door and entered the room. Morning sunlight was touching every object in the room, including an exquisitely upholstered bed. Eleanor was not in the bed. Nor was she in any other corner of the room.

Eleanor was with Alan. Of that, she was certain.

Left breathless and angry in the same instant, she—Alan's neglected wife—ran from the room in search of them. She left the house as though she were leaping away from it, compelled by the news it had imparted to go in search of her wily husband and his agreeable mistress. Influenced by the morning's radiance, she persuaded herself that Alan and Eleanor may have intended to spend a private hour lying together, compatible and intimate, on the wind-stirred beach and afterwards swimming in restless ocean waters.

When she arrived on the tawny sands of the beach, she saw them at once. No other human beings were there. A gray-backed gull was soaring with predatory aptitudes above the restless waves, in search of a blue fish or a striped bass. Above the ocean, a sun-luminous sky observed the restless waves and the flight of the ravenous gull. In the faraway distance, a chalky cliff rose out of the ocean like the white gleaming bones of a sea monster from an ancient world.

Dawn was withdrawing, casually deferring to the bright ascendance of morning. Golden hues and a roseate blush filled the azure blueness of the sky and scattered across the wind-quickened waves of the ocean. In that very instant, she saw them—Alan and Eleanor—sauntering hand in hand along the tawny sands of the beach. Eleanor was wearing a white dress and white sandals. Alan's navy polo shirt, white trousers, and navy boat shoes enhanced his casual masculinity. The virile reality of this handsome man—this prodigious mind and self-possessed individual that for nearly six years had been her ardent lover (though away on battlefields much of the time) and for five years after that her husband—this extraordinary man drew all of her attention and her inquiring witness. Exactly at that moment, Alan paused in his sauntering and influenced Eleanor to pause as well. He drew her to himself and passionately kissed her. Again and again he kissed her while his rugged arms enclosed her. She, in turn, received his kisses with the same ardency. She murmured loving words that must have declared, as an echo of all her similar murmurings, that she would love him forever.

Unobserved by them, she, Charlotte Dussolier Aubray—the wife that Alan was so causally betraying—turned away and quickly left the beach. On that morning, she did not care to make a scene or to evoke from Alan and Eleanor disingenuous self-recrimination and shame or even a willful carelessness that refuses to conceal its rebellious fervencies.

During the two or three days that followed, she gave no sign that she had discovered the intricate workings of their relationship. Instead, with the genteel affability and precise knowledge of a dedicated teacher in the spacious rooms on the second floor of the east wing that had become their school, she explored with Eleanor the ambiguities of justice in Herman Melville's novel *Billy Budd*. Together, they examined the themes of loneliness and anxiety in the Symbolist prints of the Norwegian artist Edward Munch.

They debated the causes of the First World War, including the mutual defense agreements that drew many European countries into battle; the desires of those European countries for greater empires that involved their overtaking parts of Asia and Africa; and the assassination of Archduke Ferdinand, the heir to the Austro-Hungarian throne. During the hours they devoted to trigonometry, they reviewed the Pythagorean theorem; angles of elevation and depression; tangents and slopes; right triangles and oblique triangles; and the law of sines and cosines.

Eleanor was an apt pupil. She was also immoral, self-centered, and duplicitous. Studious, creative, and blithe, she gave no evidence of having betrayed the unspoken promises of the pact that she had made with Alan and with her. Intense sex was allowable. Authentic love between Alan and her—lonely and grieving Eleanor, an eighteen-year-old impressionable young woman—was never part of the rebellious scenario that the three of them had entered.

Both teacher and confidante, she kept her counsel whenever she was in Eleanor's company. Even when, alone together, they spent an hour sailing on the breeze- tossed waters of the lake behind the main house, or when they rode their Arab bays along the horse trail that kept hastening away from the north fields behind the main house, or when they picnicked on a green hill that overlooked the lake, she maintained her decorum, yoked as it was to her even temper and her cynical awareness that human beings are a problematic species capable of devious plots and multiple betrayals.

She told herself that she must forgive Alan and Eleanor for having crossed the line of demarcation they had kept invisible—that boundary separating genuine love from illicit passion. Yet, if they continued to explore the exciting fervors of their new-found love…if, despite Alan's bond with her, his loving wife, they—Alan and Eleanor— continued to revel in the new intensities of their passion, she must discover a plan that would draw Eleanor away from him.

Another unhappy dream prodded her toward that goal.

In her dream, suddenly, without a moment's premonition so that she could push away the melancholic fear that was hovering by her, a new, uneasy sight of Alan and Eleanor rose before her imagined witness: with naked abandon they were swimming in the heated pool that was located in the south wing of the Marnham property. So real and life-like was her dream that, as before, she bolted from its maddening imagery. In that very instant, she heard herself screaming. It was a scream of protest. It was a scream of sorrow. Dawn light crossed through and past the panoramic bedroom window and showed her what she had already guessed. Alan was not sleeping next to her.

She hurried from her bed, her tall, slim figure made even more glamorous in a scalloped lace-trim dark-green chemise nightgown and matching robe. Dark green slippers enhanced her vivid presence, her being right there in the moment. Now, with renewed determination, she made her way hastily toward the comforts of the heated pool and the amenities of the pool house. Stepping inside the pool house, she observed with familiar awareness the mahogany-framed French doors, floral curtains and slipper chairs, candelabra-like chandelier, and easy access to the bluestone loggia that faced the teal waters of the pool.

No amorous couple was swimming in the pool or standing with elated gaze upon one another in front of the loggia. Only the roar of the ocean's restless waves echoing across the wind-tossed distance apart from the pool house disturbed the quiet of this place. Yet the pool house still conveyed its promise of solacing pleasures, perhaps because the glowing light of the early morning sun was touching the French doors and the floral curtains and the slipper chairs.

Where were Alan and Eleanor?

Goaded by the sting of this question, she returned to the main house dismayed as much as she was disappointed that she had not discovered the whereabouts of her husband and his protégée. Instead of entering the house from the front door, she walked along the long flower-bordered path that led her to the wide expanse of the green lawn behind the house. Dressed as she was in her dark green nightgown and matching robe, she made her way along the picturesque path, as she often had on happier early mornings, toward the gazebo that stood within its own privacies. Abiding by Gerald Marnham's wishes, Alan had designed and built a twenty-foot eight-sided oval double-roof gazebo. Providing a comforting retreat from busy obligations, the oval-shaped cedar gazebo had become for her a soothing resource. Its sectional sofa and matching chairs, its coffee table and hanging plants with red, blue, and yellow flowers, its serene sea-blues and tans, and its large windows gave the interior a homelike, sun- touched atmosphere.

She had nearly reached the gazebo when the tall, muscular body of a young man standing by a window inside the gazebo caught her attention.

Suddenly made tense once again, she stopped in her tracks. The man was leaning toward a girl who was not yet a woman and no longer merely a girl. This girl-woman was seated on the sofa next to which the man was standing. His rugged arms outstretched, the man now took hold of the girl-woman and lifted her into his passionate embrace. She looked like a princess in a white summer dress and white sandals, and he was her persuasive lover wearing with casual self-possession a navy polo shirt, white trousers, and navy boat shoes. These two—the amorous man and the consenting girl-woman—were the same couple that she had seen in her dream.

The man was Alan, her wayward husband, and the girl-woman was Eleanor.

In this quickened moment, the familiar reality that she knew heaved up and hurled away. The early morning sky swirled upward. The double-roofed gazebo and the expansive lawn billowed, eddied, and spiraled away from her. From a hazy distance, the morning waves of the ocean were rising and echoing and crashing against spume-fed air and distant chalky cliffs. Even the main house was rising and then rushing away.

She closed her eyes and stood very still. Only after she promised herself that she would make things right did she open her eyes and return to the house. Not once did she look back at the gazebo or at the romantic couple who probably were still passionately kissing each other.

"I will make things right," she told herself once more as she entered the main house. "I will do the things that need to be done. I will save the three of us."

First of all, two days later, she questioned Alan about the intensity of his feelings for Eleanor. She began by searching for the truth of his feelings about herself, the wife he had passionately loved for the five years of their marriage and for six years before that. On this Sunday afternoon, they were standing alone together in the rose garden by the blue-rimmed well, the sun-radiant place where they had first met Eleanor. She, Alan's conflicted wife, was wearing a flowered sleeveless chiffon dress with waist cutouts and cascading ruffles. Its lace-up tie-back, full-length hem, and A-line silhouette brought a glamorous emphasis to her tall and slender figure. Her royal-blue, open-toe high heel dress shoes with buckle straps enhanced the glamour. Alan was wearing a tan, basket-weave linen-silk suit and a collarless azure shirt with tan stripes. Within a few minutes, they would be on their way to a lavish party to which Gerald Marnham's neighbors a mile away had invited them. The party would probably last from mid-afternoon until after midnight. To all inquiring eyes, they would appear to be what they were not: a happily married couple. Eleanor would not be with them. She was at Saranac Lake in upstate New York, visiting one of the bright and upright friends she had made while she attended Miss Porter's School in Farmington, Connecticut.

Here, by the blue-rimmed well in Gerald's rose garden, she stood alone with Alan, their intimacy grown somewhat aloof and occasionally tense. She took the plunge. She began speaking about the truth of things. She wanted to save him from himself. She wanted to rescue Eleanor, too, and rescue herself, as well.

She began softly, always matter of fact and probing. "Something has changed between us," she told him. "Your interest in my activities and your affection for me as an up-to-the-minute person have diminished. Even your lovemaking has become less intense and is mostly non-existent. What's wrong? What has changed you? Or who?" She was urging him to make a confession. She was waiting for him to tell her the truth in the blunt and incisive manner that had become his trademark.

He did not avoid her searching eyes. He did not turn away when he spoke or devise a mock interest in the long-stemmed roses that caressed the edge of the path leading to the well. He faced her directly and declared himself with smooth intonations and confident remarks.

"It's Eleanor," he said. "She has made everything different. She has made *me* different. With her, I feel as though I am twenty years old again. I keep telling myself that I've fallen in love—*really* in love—for the first time. She has become my lifeline. She is my obsession."

"You are not twenty years old," she answered him, "and you happen to be married to me."

"I am not your prisoner," he said. "Though I am a married man, I am free to explore the world in my own way.

I am free as a young and inquiring man to make of my world the adventure that I want it to be."

"What about fidelity? What about the promises you made when we married?"

"I have to be faithful to myself first of all. We should not be shackled to our marriage. We are free to explore other relationships, even while we revise the legal agreement that married us. We can go on loving each other. At the same time, we can give our love to other partners."

To this remark, with its cynical and rebellious textures, she did not quickly respond. Alan's words were displacing the sureties of their relationship—the guarantees that kept their bond with each other both valid and successful. When she did speak, she chose words that were incisive and accusing.

"What kind of love is that? It's not profound. It's superficial. It's a will-o'-the-wisp feeling. It's not real love. Call it by its real name. It is casual promiscuity. It is self-centered gratification without sufficient thought about its effect upon your temporary partner."

He noticed her anger, harnessed though she had kept it. His brown eyes still offered her his ingrained affection. He did not want to hurt her. He wanted, instead, to tell her how it was with him. He wanted her to be a good sport. He wanted her to stay true to the unorthodox path they had chosen to follow after their hard years in the war.

"What I feel for Eleanor may not be temporary," he said. "Right now, I'm telling myself that I truly love her. Maybe my passion for her will burn out quickly. Maybe it will hold me in its spell for a long time. Whatever happens, I am in the spell right now. I am giving myself to it completely. I am giving myself to Eleanor all the way."

"What about me? Where do I fit in?"

He answered her without hesitation.

"You don't. You shouldn't even try. Leave Eleanor and me to whatever end the Fates have planned for us."

"You are telling me that we are finished."

"I don't know. I'm trying to find out. You are in my blood. I can't imagine life without you. Maybe I want you and Eleanor, too."

"Maybe you want too much. Maybe you are thinking only of *your* feelings. What about Eleanor's feelings? What about mine?"

"Both of you are free to love the way you want. You can love me alone. You can also choose to love an additional partner."

"Equally?" "Equally."

"What if I can't do that? What if I believe that your love is all that I need?"

"You have a right to stay true to your own code. But I think that you should take a temporary lover. The experience will be good for you. Already, this Eleanor episode has been very good for me. Take a lover. There will be no better proof that our love does not make prisoners of each other."

Having said so, he planted a kiss upon her cheek and, right after that, a more ardent kiss upon her lips. The press of his lips upon her own still thrilled her. With equal ardency, she returned his kiss. This mutual kissing was, she believed, their promise to maintain cordial relations. Not only was it that, a calculated rapprochement. Nor was it only a sign of their natural rapport with each another. The kiss was, she told herself, a renewal of the marriage pact that they had made five years ago. They belonged to each other, on that special day that they pledged their lives to one another and for all the days that were to follow.

There was still a chance that she could draw Alan away from Eleanor. That thought sparked her sudden elation as she and Alan now quickly left the rose garden and hurried forward to the lavish party that awaited them. She was not going to give in to his infatuation with Eleanor. She refused to be defeated by the complicated loves that were drawing them into irreversible consequences. Instead, she would devise a plan that would bring Alan back to her.

As though the kind Fates were collaborating with her, she discovered her plan the very next week. Suddenly, with only a cablegram to prepare the Newport household for his arrival, Gerald Marnham returned from his latest trip to Europe. With him he brought Brice Fontaine, the grandson of Philippe and Emmanuelle Fontaine. By chance, he and Brice had run into each other at the Hôtel Crillon on the Place de la Concorde in Paris. Within that palace setting, at the renowned restaurant L'Ecrin, they had enjoyed an excellent dinner and brisk conversation. Gerald was escorting Sylvia Blake, a glamorous, golden-brown-haired widow in her late forties—looking younger than her years—who had become more than a platonic friend. Her husband, an oil tycoon from Houston, Texas, had died the year earlier from congestive heart failure. Their two sons were now thriving executives in their father's corporation. Gerald and Sylvia were staying in luxurious suites across from each other on the second floor of the hotel. Brice, whose luxurious suite was located on the third floor, was enjoying some free time with his girl-of-the-moment.

Never one to neglect a favorable opportunity, Gerald suddenly remembered that Brice would be just the young man that Alan needed to assist him and his team in the ongoing construction of a bridge across a stream that ran through Gerald's Newport property. The summer assignment would fulfill requirements that Harvard had established for Brice's program there. In addition, Gerald would experience the pleasure of helping the grandson of

Philippe and Emmanuelle Fontaine to gain valuable experience from extraordinary and knowledgeable Alan.

Mr. and Mrs. Fontaine were friends not only of Gerald Marnham, but also of Alan and herself. Charlotte respected Philippe's success as a curator of the fashionable Courtney Art Gallery in Manhattan. She admired, too, his business acumen. He had made a fortune through his wise investments on Wall Street. His wife Emmanuelle was the epitome of well-preserved glamour and the daughter of a top executive in the Marnham Steel Corporation. Phillippe and Emmanuelle's son, Damien, and Damien's equally quick-witted wife, Adele, also filled top posts in the Marnham Corporation. Damien and Adele's older son, Justin, was happily married and at the age of twenty-seven was enjoying his career as a junior executive in Gerald's steel corporation in Pittsburgh.

Brice was their second son and, at twenty years old, a far more problematic offspring. Despite his sometimes-reckless personal life, he had achieved an impressive academic record at Harvard. Come September, he would spend his third university year not at Harvard, but as an exchange student within Alan's alma mater, École Polytechnique in Paris. She was intrigued that Brice's studies were making of him an alter ego of Alan. Gerald Marnham noticed their similarity, too. Already, he was calling Brice an extraordinary young man. Brice was, after all, training to become not only a civil engineer, an urban planner, and a landscape architect. His studies in France would also include mechanical and aeronautical engineering.

She had met Brice at some of the magnificent parties that his grandparents hosted in Newport and in Manhattan. She had also conversed and even danced with him at the elegant parties that his parents hosted when they were away from their home in Pittsburgh and were spending some vacation time in their Manhattan penthouse. On every occasion that they met, Brice impressed her with his easy-going manner, his self-assurance, and his extraordinary sandy-haired handsomeness. Standing at six foot, three inches and possessing an athletic build, he dominated every room that he entered. Whether, after being urged by partygoers to share anecdotes about himself, he was recounting his adventures kayaking on the white waters of the Tornio River in Finland or skydiving from twenty thousand feet above the foothills of the Rocky Mountains within the Eastern Plains of Colorado or riding a bay-colored Appaloosa bareback on a horse farm in North Dallas, Texas, he won approving glances from every guest.

From Rosamond Beaumont, one of her schoolfriends years earlier and now a sophisticated young woman who had seen much of the world and had met both successful and problematic people, she learned some useful information about Brice. It was well-known in privileged circles that Brice had been sexually active since he was sixteen. He had journeyed from one brief affair after another, usually with debutantes from his own class and sometimes with chorus girls and corporate secretaries. Having reached the age of twenty, he was an experienced and even generous lover. He could also be ruthless, breaking away from his girlfriends without pity or regret or even a particle of empathy.

"Brice is very clever," Rosamond said. "Maybe he is too clever. One day he may fall in love with the wrong girl. Then he will find out how terrifying love can be."

Inside the stillness of her remembering, she heard these ominous words as if Rosamond were speaking them in this very instant. She might have accepted the memory of them as a bad omen. But so convinced was she that Brice was going to be a key figure in her new plot and so intent was she on quickly launching this plot that she dismissed as irrelevant and unimportant her memory of Rosamond's warning.

She hurried forward to make of her plan a vivid reality. She was going to guide Eleanor onto Brice's path. She was going to draw Eleanor away from Alan. She was going to make certain that Brice became Eleanor's lover.

First of all, she was going to make Brice *her* lover. In that way, she would rouse Eleanor's attention and her self-centered desire to claim Brice for herself.

CHAPTER SEVEN

COMPLICITY WITH THE UNEXPECTED

At first, the Fates collaborated with Charlotte. She perceived in the events that quickly revealed their surface meanings that Gerald and Sylvia, his genteel lady, accepted as pertinent and appropriate Alan's ambitious focus upon his assignments as the new groundskeeper of the property and as the overseer of the construction of the suspension bridge above the stream that bisected the north portion of Gerald's Newport property. Only rarely did Alan join them—Gerald and Sylvia—for the summer occasions that always lifted their spirits. When he did join them, as a seasoned sailor manning a fast-moving sailboat or as a first-rate tennis player, an accomplished swimmer, and an experienced rider of a chestnut-colored Arabian stallion, he reveled quite naturally in the authentic pleasures that the day was offering him and that, with confident authority, he fully accepted. Gerald and Sylvia noticed, too, that Alan found pleasure in the company of his wife—reliable and quick-witted Charlotte, and—with guardian perceptions—in the quiet fervencies of Eleanor, paired as she often was with her grandfather Gerald and that rigidly upright gentleman's decorous lady and with a select circle of Gerald's friends.

Gerald was especially pleased that Alan was carefully mentoring Brice Fontaine, who spent most of his time working with the engineers and the builders who were constructing the suspension bridge. When Brice did socialize, Gerald was quick to observe, he was usually in the company of Alan and Charlotte, the ideal couple to whom he gave most of his dutiful attention. Though Eleanor was often in their company, Brice behaved toward her as though he were her big brother and an able guardian of her well-being. His conduct impressed Gerald and Sylvia.

"He's one of us," Gerald remarked to Alan and Charlotte as he with Sylvia and she with Alan made their way to the dance floor during the elegant birthday party that Gerald was hosting in celebration of Eleanor, his beautiful eighteen-year-old granddaughter. That her birthday had occurred a few months earlier did not diminish the summer glow of the celebration. The party was a festive highlight of Gerald's brief summer return to Newport. Another highlight was the favorable impression that Brice was making within the studious perceptions of Gerald and Sylvia.

"Brice knows how to behave because he knows how we think," Gerald remarked in that moment when he was entering the dance with Sylvia and when Charlotte and

Alan overheard him as they too entered the dance. "I'm not surprised that he behaves so well, though I am very pleased. He is, after all, a Fontaine."

In that instant, all of them were observing Brice as he danced with Eleanor. Casual and good-natured, he was describing the new Stutz Bearcat Sports Car that his parents had given him for his recent birthday. Polite and interested while he guided her across the glamorous space of the ballroom, Eleanor was listening to his description and observing with keen-eyed pensiveness his life-loving enthusiasm.

"He has won her respect," gentle Sylvia remarked as, with well-bred assurance, she moved across the dance floor with proficient Gerald. "It's wonderful to see her looking up to him with the same trust that she would give to a big brother."

Hearing these words as she and Alan were dancing next to Gerald and Sylvia, she—wily and rebellious Charlotte—believed even more firmly that the Fates were on her side. She needed to wait only a few more days before she brought Brice more intimately onto Eleanor's path. By then, after those few days had passed, Gerald, busy with his obligations as the CEO of the Marnham Steel Corporation, would hurry away to confer with his lawyers in Pittsburgh about new, international contracts and about some lucrative shipbuilding agreements with the United States

Navy.

If this birthday evening offered the promising sight of Brice dancing with Eleanor, it also offered an even more favorable augury of Brice's emerging romance with her. Suddenly, and quite unexpectedly, the Fates brought Brice and Eleanor into a far more intimate meeting than their partnering with natural rhythms on the polished floor of the glamorous Beaux Arts ballroom within the Newport country club where Gerald was a member of the board. The Fates were also kind to Charlotte when the musicians took a break from their adept playing. It was then, after she and Alan, as well as Gerald, Sylvia, Eleanor, and Brice returned to their table, that the Fates allowed her to notice that sorrow was suddenly, and altogether unexpectedly, touching Eleanor's face and touching, as well, her tremulous lips.

In this specific instant, Gerald had unwittingly served as an agent of the Fates. He had, in the course of casual and often merry conversation, happened to mention an exhilarating birthday party that Eleanor's parents—willfully promoting their reputation as ideal mother and father—had given her more than a year earlier. That birthday evening represented a precious time when tragedy had not yet challenged Eleanor's private belief that one day not so very far away, when she had attained her adult independence, she would make a loyal friend of happiness.

On this evening fifteen months later, Gerald's well-meaning remark stirred her uncertainty and her realistic awareness that she would have no opportunity to forgive her parents for their coldhearted regard of her. Nor would she have the opportunity to make amends for her secret hatred of them while they lived. Gerald's remark summoned the ghosts of her past that she thought her new-found era with Alan and Charlotte had helped her to escape. Now, in an instant and because of Gerald's well-meaning remark, those ghosts came back to haunt her. Maintaining perfect composure, she excused herself from the brisk ongoing conversation and made her way to the terrace.

All the others at the table did not notice the traceries of sorrow upon Eleanor's face. Only Charlotte noticed. She also noticed something more that was unexpected.

Moments earlier, Brice had also headed in the direction of the terrace because, Charlotte imagined, he wanted to look upon the moonlit ocean waters and breathe the freshness of the night air. She told herself that Eleanor's withdrawal from the party was not inspired by Brice's casual leave-taking. But the coincidence of their leave-taking was an unexpected occasion, a serendipitous conflation of their different intentions and, with theirs, a conflation of her own intention as well. Her awareness of what was happening thrilled her. The Fates or, possibly, Blind Chance were activating her wish that Brice enter

Eleanor's life in a more personal way. Whether Brice would catch sight of Eleanor on the spacious terrace and whether he would speak with her, Charlotte would not guess. Whether other partygoers had also sauntered or hurried to the terrace, she had no way of knowing while she remained in her place at the long, banquet table where Gerald and his group were celebrating Eleanor's birthday. Whatever was transpiring while Eleanor and Brice were standing on the terrace together or apart at the same time, she had no way of knowing unless she, too, made her way to the terrace. With this thought in mind, she made a lighthearted withdrawal from the festive group that had brought her temporary pleasure and, with decorous composure, hurried toward the terrace.

When she entered the terrace, she saw first of all the pale-yellow moon shining like a giant amulet in the midst of the darkness of the sky, the tangled array of ghostly clouds, and the silver sheen of the stars. The moon and the stars were casting their light upon the breeze-tossed waves of the ocean. Nearer than that and only while with searching eyes she stood behind a white marble column, she saw Eleanor peering at the waves and then looking upward at the moon and the stars. She could not see her face, but she did hear the sounds of her weeping, and she saw her tall, slim figure in the floral evening dress that enhanced her beauty and made her sorrow seem incongruous and surprising.

From her place behind that column, Charlotte turned from her sighting of Eleanor and now looked for the charismatic presence of Brice. With studious gaze, her eyes took in the surround of the white marble columns and flooring, the wall-pack lighting, the azure blue chairs and umbrella tables made of moisture-resistant solid mahogany and solid eucalyptus wood. Her gaze also caught the sight of potted planters profuse with scarlet red and lavender New Guinea impatiens, blue and white lobelia, dark pink hibiscus, and the cascading whiteness of sweet alyssum. Only for this moment did she allow her glance to linger upon Brice's handsome face. Though she had not yet begun an intimate acquaintance with him, she knew him well enough to understand how he thought about life in general and what he thought specifically about his brief residence here in Newport with staid Gerald Marnham and his equally conservative friends.

Brice had, she imagined, left the elegant birthday celebration feeling like a prisoner of the ambitious program his parents and grandparents had devised for his summer recess from university studies. Weary on this evening of having to fulfill the role of one of the Fontaine family's dutiful heirs, he had stolen away from the party, colored though it was with glittering surfaces, buoyant personalities, and extravagant appurtenances. He intended to absent himself only long enough to calm his vague dissatisfaction by lighting up and inhaling one of the Imperial cigarettes favored by his father and eventually by himself. The summer breeze wafting across the wide expanse of the nighttime terrace quickened his senses and mitigated, in part, the melancholy that was overtaking him in spite of the festive occasion. That he had temporarily abandoned not only the party, but also the watchful eyes of Gerald's friends intensified the rush of satisfaction that stirred his awareness of the vivid moon and of the star-filled sky in the vaulted space above him and of the efflorescent panorama of the Newport waters that sparkled in the distance.

As far as he was concerned, the essential reason for his being here in Newport was to win the approval of Gerald and Alan. Their approbation, granted only if he measured up to their high standards, would at summer's end influence his parents' belief that this brief Newport visit and his internship in the bridge-building assignment that Alan was overseeing had wrought a necessary reformation and a wise move away from the wildness that was blocking his better possibilities and tarnishing his reputation. For all these reasons, he had left the party to breathe the air and to tell himself that, if he played the right cards with his fate, he need not become absolutely the prisoner of this summer scenario that his family and Gerald Marnham had decided he must carry forward, as though he were a puppet dangling from their strings or an actor playing a role that they had arbitrarily assigned him.

As she observed him from her place behind the marble column, Charlotte imagined, as though she were a seeress who had knowledge of other people's destinies, the motives that were igniting Brice's will and the promise that he had made to himself to endure this ascetic period that his family had thrown onto his path as though it were some gauntlet from an earlier century, a glove worn with medieval armor to protect the hand and an open challenge to combat. That he had metaphorically taken up the glove, that he had in this very real year of 1923 accepted the challenge, was all in his favor. He would offer his family and Gerald Marnham—and, yes, Alan Aubray, whose proficiencies as an architectural engineer he genuinely respected—an authentic performance in the role they had created for him. With quick-witted conviction, he would become the reliable heir whose various merits always appeased his family's doubts of him. But his imitation of the life of this solid human being would be only temporary. When summer ended and, as an exchange student, he turned to his studies in Paris, he would continue to negotiate with the Fates who had usually favored his adventurous approach to life.

So Charlotte imagined as she observed Brice from

her place of concealment on the meticulously-appointed terrace just beyond the glamorous ballroom in Newport's most fashionable country club.

She understood that, when he hurried away from the party minutes earlier and entered the more private space of the terrace, Brice did not elude the party completely.

With the polished assurance that gave him a courtly manner, he had left the banquet table precisely at the moment that the musicians returned and began playing a new set of ballads. He had made his way with equal assurance and with brisk gait away from the dance floor and on to the rim of the crowded dining room, filled as it was with couples in tuxedos and gowns and made painterly by the yellow gold of dahlias, the lavender of camellias, the red of hibiscus, and the peach hues of roses that flared their beauty in precise arrangements at the center of each table. But, even when he entered the wide expanse of the terrace that had been temporarily abandoned by the partygoers who had given themselves over to the exhilarated camaraderie of the dance, the sounds of the party followed him. Behind him, as a faraway impression, the melodious rhythms of a Cole Porter love ballad were navigating the blues-jazz sounds of piano, trumpet, and violin. The smoky voice of the woman who was singing it rose with aptitudes both seductive and poignant. The voices of the guests, intermittently hushed or cacophonous, were another riff upon his senses.

Yet the merriment of the party could not displace the tremulous sounds of the girl-woman who was weeping within the shadows of a marble column not more than ten feet from where he stood, just beyond the entrance to the terrace. For a moment, he debated whether he should stay or go, so disinclined was he to become involved in the problems of this distraught girl. When she moved forward, out of the shadows that, even now, partly covered her tall, slim frame, he noticed—without yet apprehending her face—her blonde hair and young, fair-skinned arms. Still weeping, she took a handkerchief from her purse and, while she was drying her tear-stained face, she struggled to regain her composure. He might have turned from her and hurried back to the party. But right after she placed her handkerchief inside her purse once more and moved forward again to peer ruefully upon the glittering ocean, the light of the moon caught her in profile. Now, with quickened heartbeat, he saw who she was. This weeping figure was none other than Eleanor, Gerald's beautiful granddaughter.

With no hesitation, he hurried to her.

"I see that I am not the only one who appreciates the sight of the moon and the stars glowing upon Atlantic waters," he began. "The glow makes a splendid marriage of moon and sea."

She turned quickly to peer upon his face. His husky, matter-of-fact voice had startled her. She was not anticipating him or, for that matter, any other person. With the cool detachment that he recognized as the armature of her self-possession, she met his remark with clipped inflections.

"We have something in common, then, you and I," Eleanor said. "But I never imagined that you enjoyed looking up at the summer moon and the glittering stars and the breeze-tossed sea while you were alone. I know very little about you. But what I do know tells me that you prefer this here-and-now, land-bound world. The moon and the stars and the sea might be a convenient backdrop when you are with one of your girlfriends. They are a means to an end. You are not a dreamer. In that respect, you are a true Fontaine."

"Ah, but I did come here alone, and I was looking up at the moon and the stars as they sent their glow upon the sea."

"So you were."

"But I was not crying."

These words made her pause. When, after a moment, she answered him, her voice anchored its sorrow to a harder edge.

"No, you were not crying. You have no reason to cry."

"But you have."

Once again, she shrouded herself in silence. Beneath the artifice of her composure, he discerned her struggle. She was uncertain of him. She did not know whether she should explain the cause of her sorrow. Now, as if to clarify the person that his rugged demeanor represented, she looked upon him with a more studious gaze. Only then, while choosing carefully measured words that kept in check the anguish that she was experiencing, did she declare herself to him.

"I was thinking of my parents. I was remembering the good things they did for me and all the ways that I disappointed them. I was remembering, too, how little we understood each other."

"You want to hate them, but you can't. There's a part of you that still wants to love them."

His words were precise, yet blunt. They sounded uncannily accurate. The remark startled her. The probing words made her defensive. Her quick reply, weary and angry at the same time, yoked itself to the grim reality that the deaths of her parents had left her to live through.

"Of course I love them and hate them, too. But what does it matter? They are not here. They will never be here with me."

"You are going forward with your life. You are meeting new people and preparing for your future. Next year, you will begin your college days. After that, you will enter the adventurous world and the career that will bring new meaning to your life. That is a good thing."

Once more she looked pensively upon him. Only then did she accept the truth of his remark.

"Yes, it is a good thing. Alan and Charlotte and my grandfather, too, have been rescuing me. I like to believe that someday I shall be the one who rescues troubled people."

He pressed further.

"You admire Charlotte and Alan."

Her words came more quickly now, extemporaneous and matter of fact. She wanted, in this moment, to tell him how it was with her. She wanted him to understand who she was.

"I do admire them," she said. "Charlotte and Alan and I understand each other. When I first met them, I was struggling through the grief that I felt after my mother and my father died. I had heard many stories about Charlotte and Alan. I heard about their courage and their suffering. I had been told that the war had robbed them of their belief that the world would ever be anything except a secret adversary and a destroyer of aspirations. Never before had I met a man and a woman capable of battling their grief and their despair and subduing—if not altogether escaping—its powers over them. I was impressed and moved that they could grieve so profoundly and then hurry forward not to death but to life. I told myself that they and I shared the same spirit. Ironical, isn't it? Our grieving became a bond between us."

"I don't know Alan and Charlotte so very well," Brice said. "But I think that they go on grieving, though they grieve mostly in secret—even from each other."

"Perhaps my being with them makes grief bearable for them and for me," Eleanor said. "They become even more important for me on an evening like this one, when unhappy memories bring my parents back to me. Because Alan and Charlotte are here, I can turn away from my ghosts. I can go to them and, without speaking a word, they will take my hands and comfort me."

"Then, you must allow me to bring you to them," Brice told her. "Parties are not meant for ghosts."

His words were softer. They suggested his empathy. Eleanor allowed herself the hint of a smile. But melancholy did not leave her voice, and her blue eyes remained clouded with her grieving. Nevertheless, and without any reluctance, she took hold of the arm that he extended to her so that they could return to the party together.

"Yes," she said. "It is time to leave my ghosts—at least, for tonight."

He brought her back to Alan, who was sitting at the banquet table, conversing with two business partners about the stock market. From her concealed place near the threshold of the terrace, Charlotte carefully observed them. As Brice and Eleanor approached him, Alan scanned their faces. He noticed at once the rapport between them. He noticed, too, that Eleanor had been weeping. Brice's solicitous manner toward her did not in the first moments of observing them displease Alan. As a Fontaine, Brice was granting Eleanor the respect that was her due. He was doing what needed to be done. He was a true Fontaine. He was offering consolation to a melancholic girl-woman.

So Alan told himself, reluctant to believe that Brice had more than a platonic interest in Eleanor.

Yet, as the evening hurried forward to its many festive occasions, Alan grew dismayed. He had heard about Brice's casual affairs with young and older women. He well understood the arrogance and the cold-heartedness concealed within his possession of them. He and Brice were men of the same disposition. He comprehended with keen-eyed perceiving the muted desire that touched Brice's face whenever, with furtive glance, he looked upon Eleanor. On this evening, Alan concealed his displeasure. He had no plans to share Eleanor with Brice or with any other man.

But Charlotte had plans. Returning discreetly from the terrace, she had observed Alan's unease. At the same time, she believed that Alan's unease was a premature response. Brice had no plan to seduce Eleanor. In his eyes, she was a grieving innocent, a girl-woman who was not ready for a love affair. Though their meeting on the terrace had intrigued Eleanor's interest in Brice, she felt certain that Eleanor was not ready to turn away from her passionate and secret affair with Alan. Nor was Brice interested in bringing into his speckled life new complications with a sorrow-haunted girl that would alienate his parents, his grandparents, and Eleanor's grandfather, Gerald Marnham.

Brice would not disdain an affair with *her*, Charlotte Aubray—the brave nurse who had withstood the horrors of war. He would regard her as a woman wise to the world's various depredations and receptive to the vigorous lovemaking of a man ten years her junior. They would be good for each other. They would welcome their copulations as gifts from the Fates who admired men and women with adventurous dispositions and sensual appetites. She and Brice would not fall in love. They would enjoy their affair and afterwards continue their search for other pleasures. While they were enjoying each other, she would make both Alan and Eleanor aware of her passionate union with Brice. She was not certain that Alan, with his jaded disposition, would object to such an arrangement. But Eleanor might very well view her coupling with Brice in an altogether different way. Eleanor might very well become jealous. Believing so, Charlotte continued to devise the plan that would bring Brice into her bed. While she and Brice were enjoying their affair, she would initiate her plan to draw Eleanor to Brice and away from Alan.

She had to wait only a few more days before Gerald made his departure for Pittsburgh. For him, it was going to be more than a business trip. Sylvia was joining him. In addition to his business meetings, there would be upscale shopping excursions, summer concerts, and impressive art galleries in nearby Philadelphia, and boating, tennis, golf, and polo matches in Bucks County.

On the morning that he made his departure, Gerald offered her and Alan heartfelt praise.

Toward Alan, he showed unbridled enthusiasm.

"You are prodigious, my good man," he said. "You and your able assistants are turning my dream of a suspension bridge across that picturesque stream a vivid reality. You are a born leader."

She observed Alan summoning a smile worthy of a war hero and a meticulous engineer. The smile was genuine and respectful. It drew its energies from the smile that he had sometimes offered to his commanding officer after he had received recognition for meritorious conduct on horror-laden battlefields. Though Gerald was not a military officer, he was a commander of a sort. He was the wealthy boss. He was the CEO of Marnham Steel who was conscious of his social standing and wary of diminishing any of his powers, social and monetary. He was the man of the hour, the prevailing influence, and the decisive vote. He was the prestigious conservative suppressing liberal dialogues. He was the five-star general of the status quo so long as that status preserved the authority of the rich and subdued the troublemakers clamoring for more democracy.

Though he came from the same wealthy class, Alan regarded himself as one of the liberals. He disdained Gerald's prejudices and his insularity. Yet he found within himself a grudging respect for Gerald's ability to remain true to the codes that defined his exalted class and his place within it. Cynical and cunning and ambitious, Alan had, in this moment of Gerald's leave-taking, offered this distinguished gentleman—whose lovely granddaughter, Eleanor, was fulfilling his own bitter heart's passionate desires—the respectful smile that he had sometimes presented to his commanding officer during the turbulent years of war when that same commander had praised him. He also chose words that gave Gerald much pleasure.

"It is your wish for a suspension bridge and for a modernist upbuilding to your property that is inspiring my efforts," he said. "That, and the fact that your property requires a bridge and renovative additions worthy of its magnificence."

"You are the right man for the job," Gerald answered him, beaming all the while. "You are a very special man, indeed."

To her, the young woman he regarded as both competent and dedicated in all that she was doing for his granddaughter, Gerald offered equally kind words.

"You are a treasure, Charlotte," he said. "You have brought Eleanor into life again. You continue to show her how to make her world a remarkable and wonderful experience."

With forthright conviction, she gave him the answer he was seeking. Her gracious manner gave no evidence of the irony hidden within her remark.

"I am doing what you wanted me to do," she said. "I am teaching her a new way to see."

"So you are," Gerald said, pleased at her refined grace and at the propriety of her deference. "So you are."

Having said as much, he hurried away with Sylvia. Whatever problems existed in Newport were no longer his to ponder—at least not until his next return to his impressive estate.

Only now, when Charlotte was free to initiate the plot that would bring Brice to her bed and rouse Eleanor's envy and desire for the vigorous young man whom her impressionable eyes would begin to perceive as ideal, only in these swift-moving days did the Fates begin to play havoc with Charlotte's wiliness. Only now, when she was searching for ways to win back Alan's love, did the reality unfurling around her take her by surprise. The surprise lived urgently and predominantly within her immense love for Brice—a love that began to flare its powers not even a week after the evening that had belatedly celebrated Eleanor's eighteenth birthday. Within that week, she had shared with Brice many of the hours when he was free of his work with Alan and an equally proficient crew on the building of a suspension bridge across a stream located in the north section of Gerald's property.

"You are a free spirit," Brice told Charlotte while his intimate voice was holding her in its spell. "You and I are two of a kind."

They were racing across Newport waters in Gerald's Atlantic keelboat, a thirty-footer with an open-cockpit, a keel-mounted rudder controlled by a tiller, and a fixed fin keel. As they sailed across the quickened waters, she received the wind as a gift for her senses. She discovered new joy in the wind's echoing melody and in its wafting sea-fragrance. To her excited perceptions, the touch of the wind was elusive caress and cloud-driving impetus. Already the sky was discarding its blue textures and revealing with carefree spontaneity bruised grays and violets and crimsons. But the dazzle and warm lilt of late afternoon shimmered yet across her rediscovered happiness. It was granting her and this magnificent young man who was her partner the crispness of its favor and the promise of its venture-laden expectations.

She was experiencing this first hour on the bay with Brice as a series of indirections and a discovery of unexpected inclines and sinuous turnings. It seemed in the sheer lift and pulse of her enthusiasm as though they, in their sailboat leaving the shore, were disengaging themselves from essential roots and anchors and foundations. The fleet portion of the world unfurling before her heart-quickened senses was all disengagement and even dislocation. It was their complicity with the unexpected. It was a swift disjoining of earth's safer boundaries not only from the intricate transitions of the bay, but from the ballast and equilibrium of the familiar, as well. There, beyond the brine-green wake of waters whose roiling track glistened on the brisk sea's disarrangement— right there, while before the lilt and glow of her backward glance the shoreline in rapid motion eluded with an agile geometry the summer waves' wily incursions— just *there*, at the sun-glanced line where the furrowing sea arced toward the shore, the land leaped, tensile and accurate and then swerved and spun and scrolled, scattering whole houses and trees and summer people. Or so it seemed to her eager senses.

So it seemed as with comfortable acumen she eased the yawl's white-flashing jib sheets to test the wind's new, supple currents and afterwards, as limber Brice with an athlete's powers taught the mainsail to scan both risk and necessity. So to her it all so marvelously seemed in the thrill and push of her flourishing awareness that this extraordinary afternoon could find its meaning in their venturing departure from the land and in their undeclared surrender of all the places that knew them. It found its meaning as well in her leave-taking of the self she had so often compassed and, paradoxically, in her willful arrival before the convoluted mysteries of the sea and before her own mysteries and convolutions.

Now, while turning toward wind-raveling waters and sun-clasped clouds and the floating haze of chrome green hills across the bay, she noticed—as though he were a prowess as intricate as the sea—magnificent Brice Fontaine. He was hiking out over the gunwales of his craft, his ruggedness tethered by canvas straps to his yawl's brisk velocity. Vivid and actual, he was in her approving eyes like the sun-gold youth from nautical stories taming a wily dolphin or like some unknown sea god with a gift for balancing a sailboat as well as for taming ocean winds and waters. Here beside Brice while hiking with him to windward, she was discovering new happiness. Leaning assured and proprietary into hastening space just beyond their heeling vessel, she imagined in this very instant that she was rising from foam-covered waves glancing off their boat's zinc-white hull.

Impossible it was to keep but a moment, in the surging awareness of her senses, this imagery of herself and Brice as confident allies of the day's rapid processes. So smoothly did they bring their craft to a confluent swiftness and balance that the burnished imagery that in her mind's eye was themselves navigating their vessel hastened into the sun-flecked recessions of space before her, where the blue-opal distance kept spiraling backward. So much brighter than day were they to her imaginative eyes on that occasion that even the sea appeared to part its vigorous waters. It was as if for them alone together, for daring Brice and her reborn self, there grew voluminous and tactile a faster corridor hurrying them away from the lift and flare of her fleeting glance toward a territory of bold cutters and catboats, a half-dozen or more, glimmering above the churning push of darker waters.

But farther than that even, though before the pulsing skyline sloped and spun within a haze of hills—just before— there, on wind-flung waves and teeming mist, a solitary yawl rippled like flickering light, gold-orange and amber and viridian silver. Then, because new radiance above the yawl directed her attention, she saw a cadre of glaucous-winged gulls pursuing hidden curvatures of sunlight and air and rose-tinted cloud. Only minutes after that, in the flurrying distance, she glimpsed inlet and bay, greenery and grove, and the silver-blue sheen of a promontory. Yet sometimes she understood—in an instant—glint of meadow and gleam of farm-field and congregant trees stirring like celestial bodies. Suddenly, even then in this sail across the bay, she knew again as palpable and actual the hard-bodied whiteness of a waiting lighthouse. And always, while with her rugged Brice she became on rapid waters a collateral emphasis, she felt summer-warm winds spilling around them as from a sail of the quick, mysterious earth.

On this splendid afternoon and on so many other vivid afternoons during these three weeks that she had begun to know him well, she exulted in the sight of Brice's brawny assurance, the touch of his hand upon her shoulder, the press of his lips upon her lips, and the sound of his deep, confident voice. She exulted, too, and most of all on their sequestered nights together because of the vigor of his passionate thrusting and his confident stroking inside her consensual body.

She had not meant to fall in love with Brice. Falling in love with him had not been part of her plan. She imagined that she and Brice would have a brief affair and that the romantic glow of their being so often together would eventually rouse Eleanor's interest and her envy. Then, Eleanor would turn away from Alan after she quickened Brice's interest. With sated appetite, Alan would turn away from Eleanor as well. With *her*—his war-traumatized and disillusioned Charlotte—he would rekindle the passion that had once made their marriage soul-nurturing and original.

But the unexpected overtook her. The love she felt for Brice had already become a furious joy, a marvelous obsession, and a tremendous need.

With reluctance, she went forward with her plan to bring Eleanor into Brice's bed. Theirs would probably be a temporary love affair—a will-o'-the-wisp passion that quickly burnt itself away. Brice's being with Eleanor need not keep him away from *her* bed—the comforting bed of a slightly older woman whose worldly ways and war-hardened disposition intrigued him.

CHAPTER EIGHT
THE FAVOR OF THE WORLD

Charlotte *did* intrigue Brice. Away from his carnal relationships with genteel debutantes and university girls who slept around, he was looking for a love affair. He did not enjoy living the hairshirt life of a celibate or a prison-like withdrawal from the dating scene. After these few weeks in Newport, where he was involved in the challenge of building a suspension bridge, he felt an urgent need to make love to an enticing woman. The Newport girls, carefully watched by their parents, were not the answer. Nor was Eleanor the answer, at least not yet. Her grieving disposition roused his pity more than his sexual need of her. Since the overprotected Newport girls and grieving Eleanor could not join him in the passionate summer escapades that he desired and which he regarded as a rightful pleasure, he needed to look elsewhere. He was, a fatherly fortune-teller from Marrakesh had recently told him, an extraordinary human being cherished by the gods. He was an intrepid young man, a brave soul, and a Fate-defying adventurer. Already, in so many ways, he had proved his mettle, tested his endurance, and reveled in his well-honed manly capacities. With a team of Watusi natives in Rwanda, the landlocked republic lying south of the Equator in east-central Africa, he had hunted lions. In the company of a team of proficient mariners, he had effectively battled a five-hundred-pound marlin in the waters of the South Seas. With a beautiful girl from Vassar, he had experienced the thrills and dangers of tandem skydiving from a plane that was flying over the breeze-caressed fields of meadow grasses on a Yorkshire farmland. In Newport, Rhode Island, he knew a different thrill while piloting an Aeromarine 75—a passenger flying boat—and made a perfect water landing. With a team of champion polo players, he had excelled while riding a strong-bodied Criollo horse in a swift and unforgiving competition that took place in Buenos Aires. There were these and so many other ways that Brice Fontaine had proved his daring and his resilience.

The favor of the world was his for the asking.

So the fortune-teller known for the accuracy of his clairvoyance had told him. The aged seer was pleased that this bold American he deemed remarkable had already begun to lead a more-than-ordinary life. The gods who observed the deeds of men had, time after time, looked upon him as one of their own—a godlike son who looked at the face of danger without flinching and who casually flouted the outmoded rules of wary, nervous men.

The fortune-teller's words stayed with him. He regarded them as a lucky omen and a prophetic message meant only for him.

Determined to make his life an always exciting adventure, Brice often chose as his intimate partners lovely women who found joy in perilous adventures and in passionate, sensual alliances.

No, the Newport girls were not right for him. Nor was grieving Eleanor.

He responded to Charlotte in an altogether different manner. She was a free spirit. She was a lovely and experienced woman. Her experiences included her courageous behavior at the rim of battlefields as well as her realistic understanding of the rapacious world and her sensual pairing with always proficient Alan and, before him, with three or four other sexually-charged partners. His copulations with Charlotte fired his senses. He felt fully alive again. Their passionate foreplay, their fervent kisses, and their mutual consummations made him feel complete and fulfilled. Whether they were navigating Gerald's racing yacht across wind-tossed waters or flying in his own American Eagle bi-plane or spending a weekend alone together in his married brother's townhouse in East Hampton, he retrieved the sensual joy and the sexual ecstasy that his bridge-building days denied him. He found, of course, a different kind of joy in the creation of the suspension bridge above the swirling waters of the stream that bisected the north section of Gerald's Newport property. Invoking the strategies of a civil engineer gave his life purpose and challenged his creative impulses. That kind of achievement gave him pleasure. But he needed more than that. He needed to feel his athletic body touching the soft body of a young woman. He needed to enter that body and, with vigorous strokes, bring her to the swooning pitch of orgasm and bring himself to the prolonged ecstasy of his own climax.

Charlotte was the answer. Wise to the errant ways of the world and to her own errant ways, she was the ideal partner. From the start, he imagined that they would not fall in love with one another. They would enjoy each other's company, take pleasure from their adventurous excursions, and revel in the love-making rhythms of their bodies. After a few weeks, after they had become sated with their adventures and their copulations and after they had wearied of each other's company, they would go their separate ways.

So Brice told himself.

Or, rather, Charlotte imagined that he told himself. Brice was too complicated for her to fathom all of his thoughts. She did not hold that against him. His enigmatic character pleased her. It challenged her perceptions. It convinced her that Brice was no ordinary man. It suggested that he and Alan were created from the same manly pattern. "I like you because you are athletic and because you are younger than I am," she casually remarked to Brice on a Sunday morning when they were spending one of their weekends together, sailing and swimming in East Hampton. "I like you especially because you are handsome and because you excite me. You are adventurous, too, and unpredictable."

She paused, as though she were carefully evaluating the truth of her words. Then, believing that a few more words would lend credence to all that she was saying, she chose other words to clarify her meaning.

"You and my keeper are the same breed of man. Yet there is nobody else like either one of you. There are so many times that I am convinced that I know all the important things about both of you. Then, like my keeper—like Alan—you do or say something that tells me I know very little about either one of you."

He had risen from their bed and had drawn open the curtains to the panoramic terrace window to allow the July sunlight to float its radiance into this well-appointed room within the second story of the East Hampton house that his married brother, who spent most of his time in Pittsburgh where he was a junior executive in the Marnham Steel Corporation, allowed him to use whenever he wished.

At the terrace door, he could feel the warm glow of the sun touching his naked muscularity and bringing to its strength an artful emphasis. In the far distance, a sun-touched mountain rose, massive and proprietary, toward a pale-blue sky and toward wind-blown fluffy clouds. Its quartz peak, nearly eight hundred feet he guessed, was jutting high above the rippling waters of a lake. Across the wide expanse of that lake, young men and women were racing their bullet-swift boats, their evanescent forms so many flashes of shimmering colors within the summer scene.

Hearing Charlotte's words, Brice turned to gaze upon her once more. Their morning sex had left him contented and even newly energized, the festering wounds of his temporary abstinence eased by the prolonged thrill of their consummation.

Charlotte was lolling against a galaxy of pillows, while the scented satin sheets that she tossed aside only partially concealed the seductive curves of her naked body. With a young man's appreciation of feminine beauty, he carefully studied her voluptuous form. That she was his secret paramour pleased him. From her, there was no post-coital guilt or self-absorbed regret that she had given herself to a man who refused to impose spiritual subtexts upon lovemaking or to confuse the heady pleasures of copulation with forever-after pledges of faithfulness. Charlotte was, he imagined, reasonably happy in her marriage to Alan, and he with her. He was unaware that Alan had strayed from faithfulness and was enjoying Eleanor's young body and her adulation. But he was aware of Charlotte's world-weary perceptions and her need to steal from the equivocating Fates as much pleasure as her wiliness allowed.

He liked the look of Charlotte as she lolled against the multi-colored pillows. She might have been a well-paid model posing for calendar art or for a museum canvas or an even better-paid call girl whose morning copulation had left her satisfied. On this specific morning, she was even more carefree, because she was toppling the rigid conventions of marriage and, he guessed, because she was avenging herself against Alan, who had become so focused upon his career that he had been neglecting his wife. That she considered Alan and him as the same breed of men, amused him, even as her remark prodded his cynical view of himself and his idealized estimate of Alan.

"Don't be too sure that your keeper and I are the same," he said. "Give Alan his due. Recognize his virtues. One of those virtues is his fidelity to you. Faithfulness has never been one of my virtues. Nor can I imagine that it ever will be."

Charlotte laughed, her green eyes brighter with exhilaration, and her moist lips and gleaming teeth enhancing her smile.

"My keeper has never been faithful," she said. "I have never held that against him, because his responses to other women have always been superficial and self-centered."

Her words impressed Brice. He wanted to know more.

"You never stopped loving him even then, when he turned to other women?"

His inquiring response pleased Charlotte. She wanted to tell him more. She wanted to tell him the whole of it. She wanted to waken his clarity.

"Alan's brief affairs have been his way of quickening his interest in me," she said. "I am the woman who challenges his intellect. I am the soulmate who never asks for pity or refuses forgiveness. I am the pal that can weather the storms and, if need be, fight my own battles. I am the woman whose love he really needs and will never leave him, no matter how many temporary girls he sleeps with or how many times he strays from society's rules about marriage."

"You are a rarity," Brice said. "You think like a matter-of-fact realist, not like a dream-laden romantic."

His appraisal pleased Charlotte. She hurried to tell him more.

"Until now, I've never felt the need to complain. I've always felt that my keeper is terrific. After all, Alan is as young and as daring as I am. In so many important ways, we think alike. We have always enjoyed resisting society's repressive conventions. Being repressed or conventional is not in our blood. We are made for more exciting responses."

"Bully for you!" Brice declared. "First-rate, and exactly my style! We three think alike. Sex and money and adventure — they are what we are made for."

Hearing his words, Charlotte laughed an exhilarant laugh. The sheer pleasure in her laughter was her way of cheering their subversive temperaments.

"We are not afraid of telling the truth—you and Alan and I. We call a spade a spade."

All this while, Brice had stood by the terrace door. The soft morning sunlight and the cool breeze were caressing his naked body and pleasing his acute senses. He was also pleased to hear Charlotte choosing words that clarified who she was even as she discovered words that, yoked though they were to conjecture, clarified who in her eyes the man that Alan was and the man that he, Brice Fontaine, was as well.

Something more stirred his interest. While explaining her freewheeling relationship to her husband, Charlotte had admitted that she had no cause to complain until now. That phrase *until now* needed further clarifying. Those two words carried the burdens of ambiguity and doubt. They hinted that something or someone was altering the unorthodox pact that Alan and Charlotte had attached to their marriage.

Brice wanted to know more. Streetwise and intuitive, he sensed that Charlotte wanted to talk about this unexpected rift between her and Alan. Suddenly, as though it was a clarifying certainty, he understood Charlotte's primary motive for spending the weekend with him, here in East Hampton. She needed to tell him about this problem involving Alan. She needed him to help her resolve it.

He walked back to the bed, his tall and husky manhood a preening emphasis upon Charlotte's steady gaze. After climbing in next to her, he fondled her ample breasts and then, with his big, powerful hands, gently caressed her face. Only after that did he touch her lips with a kiss.

"A moment ago, you said that you never felt the need to complain about your relationship with Alan until now. Tell me about it," he said. "Tell me what has changed between you and Alan. Tell me all of it because you want to tell me. Tell me because that is the primary reason you've arranged this weekend alone with me."

She pulled away from him now. Her face expressed neither displeasure nor approval. Her level glance and her even-tempered inflections suggested her matter-of-fact recognition of a marital problem that needed to be resolved. Her incisive awareness of the world's ironies and deceptions was her stay against confusion and against any emotion that could dispel the afterglow of the hour they had just shared. Their conversing here in this bedroom, about the husband whom she loved—a war-ravaged man in his early thirties who was using a much younger woman for his self-centered purposes—did not unsettle her. At any other time, the irony of the situation might have drawn her derisive laughter. But to laugh at her own hardheartedness or at Brice's jaded receptivity to all that she represented might have disarranged her composure. Instead, she grew very still.

The stillness that came upon her did not disturb Brice. Already, she imagined, he felt that he knew her well. Her silence was a strategy for taking control of the moment. After reaching for one of her imported cigarettes from the gold cigarette case on a bed table nearby and after bringing it to the flame of a gold lighter, she leaned once more into the galaxy of pillows that, in a minor way, extended the comforts of the morning. She took a few drags on her cigarette and watched the smoke wafting around them. Once or twice, she looked at him, the intensity of his blue eyes and the warmth of his solid flesh a vivid presence beside her. All this while she lingered within a silence as natural as it was reflective. He joined her in the silence, unwilling to hurry her into the words that he was waiting to hear. When, at last, she did speak, she did not refrain from mentioning where they stood with each other.

"I am using you," she said. "But you don't mind. We use one another, and the games we play always leave us happy. This weekend, though, isn't really about us—at least, not all of it. We are here together because I need you to rescue Alan from his infatuation with Eleanor."

Hearing these words, Brice at first said nothing. He sensed that Charlotte wanted to say more.

In the next moment, Charlotte told him what he needed to hear.

"Right now, Alan regards Eleanor as the magical girl who can help him to be the Alan Aubray that existed before the war—the Alan that believed happiness would be his loyal friend and that his life would always be an enjoyable adventure."

Though her words about Alan's infidelity caught him by surprise, Brice gave no evidence of startlement or even disappointment. Knowing more about Alan—knowing that he had taken an eighteen-year-old girl as his mistress—persuaded him to adjust, though not cancel, his idealized estimate of Alan Aubray. In so many ways, Alan had proved that he *was* an extraordinary man. He had been a hero on the savage fields of battle. With bayoneted rifle, he had ripped away the eyes and throats and brain cells of his enemies. He had torn open their chests and pierced through their hearts. With damaged soul, he had consented to the death inflicted by his bayonet and by his rifle's bullets. He had welcomed the sight of moist cells scattering from the brains of young men and the deep red blood gushing from their foreheads and mouths and hearts. With their own bayonets and rifles, they had not killed him. He had killed them. He reveled in his primacy.

He was a man who refused to be made a plaything of the Fates. They noticed his arrogant dismissal of the always returning horrific war memories that clung to his awareness. Time and time again, the Fates approved of Alan's hardheartedness and his determination to walk tall with tight-lipped authority and surly defiance against every kind of adversary.

The Fates admired the brusque way that Alan resisted sentimentality and the brisk manner in which he continued to acquire a keen-minded understanding of the world's deceptions and betrayals. In spite of the formidable obstacles set on his path, he was making his presence known in the world. He was a proficient engineer and a gifted landscape architect. He was a daring pilot and an equally daring sailor. He was a first-rate polo player, an avid golfer, and a medal-winning boxer. He was a husband who had created a compatible and even passionate relationship with his wife. Together, they had created freewheeling subtexts and daring privacies within the scenario of a marriage that allowed brave self-exploration and spirited adventuring. That he sometimes strayed from the promises he had made on the day that he was married did not diminish the value of his marriage or his originality or his many achievements.

So Brice believed.

Intuitive and wise, Charlotte rightly guessed what Brice was thinking. She waited for him to speak. She was counting on his helping her to push forward her plan to draw Eleanor away from Alan.

In the next minute, Brice did speak. His words interrogated her without promising the rescue that she was seeking.

"What can I do to help? How can *I* rescue Alan from his infatuation?"

"Persuade Eleanor to fall in love with you. Make her believe that you are the only man she could ever really love."

Brice frowned.

"You are asking the impossible," he said. "Eleanor believes that Alan is her rescuer. She will regard me as an intruder."

"You can do it," Charlotte insisted. "You can make her fall in love with you."

"You are asking me to play with fire," Brice said. "Eleanor is a fragile soul. If I make the wrong moves, she might break apart."

"She's the one who is making the wrong moves. She's sleeping with my husband."

"With your permission."

"Not anymore. She's gone too far. She's convinced herself that she has fallen in love with Alan."

"Maybe she does love him. Maybe she believes that she cannot live without him."

"We will know what she believes after you make a play for her. Maybe you will convince her that she will never be happy without you."

With a careful gaze that seeks to know more about the woman upon whom his gaze falls, Brice took in the whole reality of her—the titian hair flowing generously across her shoulders, the steady gaze of her wily, green eyes, the upturned nose, the moist lips, the voluptuous naked figure with the well-rounded breasts, the tempting vagina, and the long legs that, during their exciting trysts and with such feminine sensuality, wrapped themselves around the thrust of his hips.

He appreciated this woman. Her realistic take on the world complemented his own cynicism. But right now, in this instant when she was plotting the course that might bring Alan back to her, she seemed to be losing her proper bearings. This scenario that she was imagining for Eleanor and for him could not, he believed, compass her aims. It could not bring her through the destination she was imagining for herself.

After gazing upon her with studious eyes, he turned from her and hurried out of the bed. He grabbed the robe that was hanging over the arm of a richly upholstered sofa nearby and quickly covered his nakedness. After that, he took a cigarette from an eighteen-carat gold case and, with a matching lighter, brought a flame to the cigarette. He took a drag, exhaled, and once again walked to the terrace window. The sun was still sending its gleaming rays upon the granite surface of the mountain. A black-backed gull was, as one of the planet's many predators, circling the lake's blue, scintillant waters in search of an ample fish. Two speedboats were racing each other, their shimmering whiteness merging with the sheer velocity of their swiftness and with the dare-deviltry of their young laughing captains.

With reflective stillness that concealed his conflicted feelings, Brice observed this busy scene. Then, after a few minutes, he turned and walked back to Charlotte, who was still resting her body against a galaxy of comfortable pillows. Facing her directly, he asked another pressing question.

"What happens afterward, when Eleanor finds out that I do not love her?"

His question did not unsettle Charlotte. It drew from her a matter-of-fact response that held in perfect balance its bitter experience and its hard-won knowledge of the world. "She'll move on to the next chapter—a bit older and a bit wiser."

Now, with husky, temperate voice, Brice lodged a protest.

"I still say that, if things don't go her way, Eleanor might break apart. How do you think she will feel if I push Alan out of her life and, shortly afterward, walk away from her?"

"She will survive. She is one of us. She has a hard heart and a self-protective disposition. Besides, you will be freeing her from Alan, who is not the real answer for her problems or even the prince of her dreams who will bring her happiness that lasts."

"What about Alan's feelings? With me during these past weeks, he's been a straight shooter. I don't like working against him."

"You will be doing him a favor. Eleanor is not the remedy for his sorrows. She's a temporary fix. I am the only woman who has a chance to make Alan whole again. I'm the tough-minded advocate who has always loved him. I'm the miracle woman who can put together the broken pieces and make his life bearable at least most of the time. Sometimes, I can even make our lives together almost new."

For a few moments more, Brice continued to study Charlotte. With awakened clarity, he perceived new layers of her hard-grained willfulness and her inveterate insolence as she negotiated with the Fates who, he imagined, were often her friends and sometimes her adversaries.

Now, while she took another drag on her cigarette and while coils of smoke rose and wafted around her, he spoke the words that reviewed the scenario she had carefully plotted.

"You want me to take Alan's place with Eleanor. You want *me* to be her miracle man. You want me to keep her from breaking apart."

"You can do it," Charlotte said. "You can make Eleanor aware that she is just like us. You can show her how not to break apart."

Before he answered her, Brice stood very still. He reflected upon the challenge that Charlotte had delivered to him. In the same instant, he remembered the fortune-teller from Marrakesh and the message that aged man had brought to him. The Fates who controlled the destinies of all men and all women had selected him as a most fortunate human being. In every one of his pursuits and in every adventure, he was always going to win the favor of the world.

Now, because the challenge that Charlotte had carefully explained suddenly appealed to him, he spoke the words that she was waiting to hear.

"I'll go a few rounds with Eleanor," he said. "Let's see what happens."

Charlotte was pleased that Brice was in the game now.

CHAPTER NINE
AWAKENED CLARITY

"You and I are free spirits," Brice told Eleanor while his husky, insinuating voice was inviting her to explore all of life with him. "You and I are meant for adventuring together."

Eleanor brightened with anticipation. That her life could become a continuing adventure appealed to her self-centered view of the world and corresponded with the imaginary scenarios that invariably placed her in the center of exhilarating risk and daring achievement.

"Maybe we will always adventure together," she answered him. "Time will tell. At any rate, I crave excitement. I yearn for adventure."

Charlotte recognized in Brice's words to Eleanor an echo of the promises he had made to her, cynical and self-knowing Charlotte, a few weeks earlier. With her, the casual married paramour who had fallen in love with him, he had fulfilled those promises and would even now be fulfilling them. But during these recent days he had been carrying forward the plan to steal Eleanor away from Alan. In this very moment and with carefully modulated charisma, he was capturing Eleanor's attention. He was finding his way into her heart. The lasting success of his journey was not yet certain. But his confident words and his newly discovered feelings made his passage easier. The words and the feelings intensified the possibility of lasting success. He had already begun sleeping with her.

So Charlotte believed, studying with ambivalent regard the alterations within Eleanor's perception of Brice and observing as well the quiet surprise and even quieter elation within Brice's awareness of the vivacious young woman that Eleanor had become. For the very first time, he was falling in love. The experience was thrilling him. He had never felt so happy.

Once again, because it had become an enjoyable pastime, they were racing across Newport waters in Gerald's Atlantic keelboat, the thirty-footer with an open-cockpit, a keel-mounted rudder controlled by a tiller, and a fixed fin keel. With no words to explain her intimate association with Brice, Charlotte had invited Eleanor to join them. There was no need for her to explain her friendship with Brice. Intuitive and keen-minded, Eleanor had on previous occasions noticed their heartfelt glances upon one another, the ardent touch of their hands upon each other's shoulders, and the careful intimacy of their bodies standing together on the deck as they looked out at the unfurling waves of the ocean.

During those remarkable times, she—the seductive woman with an open marriage—had stood as if enchanted with prodigious Brice as they caught sight of the subtle harmonies of Nature and its even subtler dangers. What she had sighted then came swiftly back to her, though not always in the same ways or with the same implications.

This time, as the three of them sailed across the quickened waters, Charlotte noticed that Eleanor and Brice were receiving the wind as a gift for *their* senses. Their responses to the wind simulated her own, though they belonged to themselves alone and, as interesting variants, to themselves together. Their happy faces convinced her that they, together, were discovering new joy in the wind's echoing melody and in its wafting sea-fragrance. To their excited perceptions, the touch of the wind must have been elusive caress and cloud-driving impetus. Did they notice that the sky was discarding its blue textures and revealing with carefree spontaneity bruised grays and violets and crimsons? Surely, the dazzle and warm lilt of late afternoon shimmered yet across their newly discovered happiness. It was granting this impressionable girl and this magnificent young man who wanted to be her partner forever the crispness of its favor and the promise of its venture-laden expectations.

She stayed out of their way. She allowed them a

private space. She wanted Eleanor to experience this special hour on the bay with Brice as a series of indirections and a discovery of unexpected inclines and sinuous turnings. She hoped that in the sheer lift and pulse of their enthusiasm they, too, were imagining that in this sailboat leaving the shore they were disengaging themselves from essential roots and anchors and foundations. Did they comprehend as she did that the fleet portion of the world unfurling before their heart-quickened senses was all disengagement and even dislocation? They were leaving behind the terrain that they knew so well. They were making their way across the restless sea, and at the same time they were navigating their own restless spirits and the unexpected happenings that were coming their way. Possibly, their complicity with the unexpected would make plausible the tremendous change that was already beginning to influence their lives. This sailing adventure that brought Brice and Eleanor together in a new way was for them, Charlotte told herself, a swift disjoining of earth's safer boundaries not only from the intricate transitions of the bay, but from the ballast and equilibrium of the familiar, as well.

During this extraordinary afternoon, Charlotte noticed what Eleanor was now perceiving with awakened clarity. It replicated her own experience from times past.

There, beyond the brine-green wake of waters whose roiling track glistened on the brisk sea's disarrangement—

right there, while before the lilt and glow of Eleanor's backward glance the shoreline in rapid motion eluded with an agile geometry the summer waves' wily incursions — just *there*, at the sun-glanced line where the furrowing sea arced toward the shore, the land leaped, tensile and accurate and then swerved and spun and scrolled, scattering whole houses and trees and summer people. Or so it must have seemed to Eleanor's eager senses.

So it seemed to her, care-riven Charlotte, as with comfortable acumen Eleanor eased the yawl's white-flashing jib sheets to test the wind's new, supple currents and afterwards, as limber Brice with an athlete's powers taught the mainsail to scan both risk and necessity. So to Charlotte it all so marvelously seemed in the thrill and push of her flourishing awareness that this extraordinary afternoon could find its meaning in Brice's and Eleanor's venturing departure from the land together and in their undeclared surrender of all the places that knew them. The afternoon was finding its meaning as well in their leave-taking of the selves they had so often compassed and, paradoxically, in their willful arrival before the convoluted mysteries of the sea and before their own mysteries and convolutions.

Now, while turning toward wind-raveling waters and sun-clasped clouds and the floating haze of chrome green hills across the bay, Eleanor noticed what she—

Charlotte Aubray, her wily mentor—had often seen and was seeing now. As though he were a prowess as intricate as the sea, agile Brice Fontaine was hiking out over the gunwales of his craft, his ruggedness tethered by canvas straps to his yawl's brisk velocity. In Eleanor's approving eyes, he must have seemed like the sun-gold youth from nautical stories taming a wily dolphin or like some unknown sea god with a gift for balancing a sailboat as well as for taming ocean winds and waters. She, amorous Charlotte gazing upon Brice, had received him as that sun-gold youth. Surely, Eleanor saw in his masculine perfection—imagined or actual—that same heroic youth. Her glowing face and air of exhilaration revealed her feelings. Here, beside Brice while hiking with him to windward, Eleanor was discovering new happiness. Leaning assured and proprietary into hastening space just beyond their heeling vessel, did Eleanor imagine in this very instant that she was rising from foam-covered waves glancing off their boat's zinc-white hull?

Charlotte wondered while melancholy tinged her awareness that Brice was falling in love with Eleanor and that he was abandoning *her*, Alan's conflicted wife who could no longer imagine her life without him or without Brice.

Impossible it was to keep but a moment, in the surging awareness of her senses, this imagery of Eleanor and Brice as confident allies of the day's rapid processes. Uneasy because of this suggestion of intimacy between them, she noticed nevertheless how smoothly they brought their craft to a confluent swiftness and balance. The burnished imagery that in her mind's eye was themselves navigating their vessel hastened into the sun-flecked recessions of space before her, where the blue-opal distance kept spiraling backward. So much happier on this day were Brice and Eleanor to her imaginative eyes that even the sea appeared to part its vigorous waters only for them. It was as if for them alone together, for daring Brice and venturous Eleanor, there grew voluminous and tactile a faster corridor hurrying them away from the lift and flare of her fleeting glance toward a territory of bold cutters and catboats, a half-dozen or more, glimmering above the churning push of darker waters.

Together, as though they were already well-matched lovers, they saw the pulsing skyline slope and spin within a haze of hills. They saw, as well, a solitary yawl rippling like flickering light, gold-orange and amber and viridian silver, on wind-flung waves and teeming mist. Then, because new radiance above the yawl directed her attention, they saw what she had seen many times before and was seeing now, alive and kinetic in this here-and-now reality: a cadre of glaucous-winged gulls pursuing hidden curvatures of sunlight and air and rose-tinted cloud. Only minutes after that, in the flurrying distance, the three of them glimpsed inlet and bay, greenery and grove, and the silver-blue sheen of a promontory. Perhaps Eleanor and Brice understood in an instant, as she had understood on previous afternoons and was comprehending now—glint of meadow and gleam of farm-field and congregant trees stirring like celestial bodies. In this sail across the bay, did Eleanor and Brice know again as palpable and actual the hard-bodied whiteness of a waiting lighthouse? Whenever rugged Brice had sailed alone with her, the conflicted wife who needed two lovers, they together—Charlotte and Brice—had become on rapid waters a collateral emphasis. As though she were living through a dream, she had felt summer-warm winds spilling around them as from a sail of the quick, mysterious earth.

It was only a matter of time before Eleanor would fall in love with Brice. Already, her interest in him was roused in a new way. Soon, she would regard him as the man she was fated to love and, possibly, to marry. Very soon, on a splendid afternoon as this one and on so many other vivid afternoons when she had begun to know him well, Eleanor would exult in the sight of Brice's brawny assurance, in the touch of his hand upon her shoulder, in the press of his lips upon her lips, and in the sound of his deep, confident voice. She would exult, too, and most of all on their sequestered nights together because of the vigor of his passionate thrusting and his confident stroking inside her consensual body.

She, the self-aware wife who resisted worn-out conventions and tyrannical moralists, had exulted in Brice's prowess as a lover and in his daring individuality. She exulted now in his brawny presence.

In the privacies of her heart and in the secret chambers of her soul, Eleanor was beginning to exult, too.

She had wanted Eleanor to fall in love with Brice. Eleanor's falling in love with him had been part of her plan. But she had not anticipated that Brice would fall in love with Eleanor. She imagined that Brice would have a brief affair with Eleanor. The romantic glow of their being so often together and the excitement of their copulations would persuade Eleanor to turn away from Alan. With sated appetite, Alan would turn away from Eleanor as well. With *her*—his war-traumatized and disillusioned Charlotte—he would rekindle the passion that had once made their marriage soul-nurturing and original. After that happened, Brice would walk away from Eleanor. One day, perhaps when she and Alan spent a few weeks in Paris or, later, when Brice began his senior year at Harvard, he—wily and passionate Brice—would return to the secrecies of his affair with her, Charlotte Aubray, whose sensual appetite required the love of two men.

But the unexpected overtook her.

Brice was falling in love with Eleanor. His fervent gaze upon her face, the ardent touch of his hands upon her hands whenever he guided her passage to a safe path or into an elegant country club, and the husky timbres of his voice as he spoke to her—all these responses became signs and emblems of his affection, his desire, and his yearning.

Eleanor was falling in love with Brice, as well, though she had not yet consented to the feelings that made her quietly uneasy and secretly delighted. Loving Brice meant that she might have to forsake Alan. She was not willing to do that. She was weighing the possibility that she might have two lovers at the same time.

Charlotte saw through her. She guessed rightly about her wayward responses. In some ways, she and Eleanor were sisters under the skin. But Eleanor was not yet comfortable with her feelings. She had not yet purged herself of her little-girl responses to reality. Nevertheless, the question of what she must do to keep the love of both Alan and Brice pushed her forward. Or rather, it was a question shrewdly posed that pushed her forward. She asked Brice the question. Right now, here in a speeding boat and inside the intricacies of that question, she chose to speak about a subject that was intensifying their longing for one another. She began speaking about love and its complicated obligations.

"Why should fidelity to one partner be the only

prescription for love?" Eleanor asked Brice. "Why can't men and women agree that there are other valid claims for love?"

For a moment or two, Brice reflected upon her questions. He perceived the soul-searching inclinations that led Eleanor to ask them. His quiet appraisal of them suggested his own soul-searching.

So Charlotte imagined, as she witnessed this exchange between them.

When Brice offered his answer to those questions, he was forthright and persuasive.

"A man and a woman whose love is authentic pledge themselves to each other and to nobody else. They do not feel the need for an additional partner. They—the two of them together—complete one another. Seeking other partners betrays the pledge they made to each other. It diminishes their love. It may even destroy it."

His words held Eleanor's attention, and they surprised her. Though he expressed himself with matter-of-fact assurance, his words suggested that the speaker was a sensitive and caring man. They hinted that Brice Fontaine was far more profound than the carefree and self-centered adventurer she had thought him to be only a few weeks earlier. Nevertheless, she challenged and tested his unexpected sensitivity and his new-found belief that fidelity to one's partner was the only accurate test of love.

"Fidelity may be overrated," she said. "If two people really love each other, they should accommodate each other's desire for an additional partner. That partner may bring temporary pleasures that actually strengthen the value that a husband and a wife confer upon one another. The arrangement can persuade a wife to look at her husband with new eyes. A husband may rediscover his wife as a special gift and even a blessing."

"That is a dangerous game they are playing," Brice said. "Usually, a game like that leaves nobody happy."

"Alan and Charlotte are happy," Eleanor quickly answered him. "Alan is playing that game with me, and Charlotte is playing it with you. No one is unhappy."

"We are playing with fire," Brice said. "Someone is bound to get hurt."

Eleanor met his new words with a momentary stillness. Was it melancholy or apprehension that took hold of her just for that moment, until she pushed it away?

Brice wondered.

So did Charlotte.

But it was Eleanor who tried to dispel the warning that Brice was delivering to her.

"Nobody will get hurt," she said. "Not if we believe that it is a game. Not if we know that it's not the real thing."

Brice's gaze was taking hold of Eleanor, possessing the whole splendid sight of her and finding a thrilling sustenance in her beauty.

Charlotte noticed and with ambivalent awareness grew uneasy.

But it was Brice who had more to say.

"What happens if you really fall in love with Alan? Or if he falls in love with you? What happens after that?"

Eleanor laughed a lighthearted laugh that enhanced her decorous charm and the elegant self-possession that only recently she had made her friend.

"I do love Alan," she confessed, "but I am not certain that I am *in love* with him."

Hearing her words, Brice seemed relieved. But he needed to know more.

"Does Alan love you?" he asked.

Once again, Eleanor laughed a lighthearted laugh.

"I'm Alan's plaything," she said. "I'm nothing more than that. Yet what I am to him is important to both of us. It fills an emptiness. It answers a need. It's a wonderful relationship because it steals none of our freedom. We are lifted by one another. Yet we are burdened by none of the encumbrances that spoil partnerships that play as though they are prison sentences."

Brice probed further.

"Is that what you believe being in love means? Being condemned to a prison sentence?"

"We are not in love with one another," Eleanor answered him, defining once again her relationship with Alan. "We are playing a beautiful game."

Now Charlotte came into it. She wanted to nudge Eleanor toward the right direction. She wanted to activate the response that lay deep within the corners of Eleanor's mind, dormant and untested. She wanted to ask the question that Brice had not asked, though that question was goading the startlement of his new perception of Eleanor and the wonderful thrill of his unexpected love of her.

"What if you discovered that someone was in love with you?" Charlotte now asked Eleanor. "What then?"

Eleanor hesitated. Apparently, she had never contemplated the experience of being in love—really in love, completely, honestly, and authentically.

"I can't say," she answered after she pushed her hesitation away. "I won't know how I feel until I feel it."

Now Brice came into it again. His question was searching Eleanor's soul.

So Charlotte imagined, understanding that in these weeks when he was carrying out the plan she had made with him Brice had fallen in love with Eleanor.

"Would you try to fall in love with the man who was in love with you?"

"Yes, I think I would try," Eleanor said after another pensive moment. "I would try very hard."

In this way, Eleanor and Brice began a new phase in their relationship. The days and weeks of their summer moved with swift ease most of the time and sometimes with urgent self-questioning and just as urgent longing. Brice continued to excel in his work with Alan on the design and building of the suspension bridge that was going to provide a safe passage above and across the stream that ran through the north section of Gerald Marnham's property. With Charlotte as her teacher, Eleanor explored—among many compelling subjects—the uneasy collaboration between environment and personal will within the characters of the Victorian novelist Thomas Hardy as they appear in *The Return of the Native, Jude the Obscure,* and *Far from the Madding Crowd.*

"Even when Hardy's characters seem to make the right choices, their environments work against them," Eleanor remarked after reading Hardy's novels.

Charlotte agreed.

"Environment—the personal space we call our home and the larger space that looms forth as our city or our country—can become our most dangerous adversary," she said. "The Hardy characters who succeed learn how to collaborate with their environments. They compromise, but at a heavy cost to themselves. They lose the spark that made them distinctive. They capitulate to societal norms. By so doing, they often lose their original selves. But, shackled though they are by those norms, they go on living. The rebels, the characters who challenge those norms, are often punished."

"I'd rather be a rebel," Eleanor said. "I want to defy every rule that hampers my freedom."

Hearing her remark, Charlotte smiled. But on that day, in the quiet of the spacious room in the east wing of Gerald's home that served as their school, she offered Eleanor words that sounded sensible and that proved to be prescient.

"Defying every hampering rule is a daring thought." Charlotte said. "But keep in mind that nothing comes free. We have to pay for the privilege of living free. We have to pay for our mistakes and even for our achievements."

"I'll keep that in mind," Eleanor promised, "especially when I am breaking free of rules."

Later, on a day when Charlotte and Eleanor were visiting art galleries in Newport, New Haven, and Boston, they became especially intrigued by the nineteenth-century American artist Winslow Homer's painting entitled *The Fox Hunt*. In that wintry scene, a flock of starving crows descends upon a fox, whose escape is slowed and probably prevented by deep snow.

"That is an especially startling scene," Eleanor said, somewhat disconcerted by the painting. "We don't often connect the fox with the role of the innocent victim."

"Winslow Homer shows us that even a wily fox can sometimes be innocent. Even a fox can become a victim."

Eleanor mused upon her remark. Only then did she reveal the truth of her feelings.

"I intend never to be a victim," Eleanor said. "I am finished with that. I was the victim of parents who pretended to love me. I was the victim of teachers who brain-washed me with their rigid rules. I shall not be the victim of a society that takes away my freedom to create myself as the person I want to be."

The audacity of her remarks pleased Charlotte. Nevertheless, she repeated her warning.

"Remember that freedom never comes free."

The summer days continued to offer useful lessons and exhilarating occasions. During these happy weeks, Brice fell more deeply in love with Eleanor. With emotions that were honest and impassioned, Eleanor fell in love with Brice. Sometimes with Charlotte and often alone together now, they went swimming in the blue-green waters of the pool within the south wing of Gerald's home. From an airfield in Warwick, Rhode Island, about forty miles from Newport, they went parachuting from an Armstrong Whitworth Atlas biplane. Along a trail a half-mile away from Gerald's home and still a part of his property, they raced their Arabian stallions with swiftly proficient horsemanship. At four extravagant parties within the Newport Country Club, Brice danced only with Eleanor. Their life together seemed to be a special gift that the fates had planned for them.

"You are my inspiration," Brice told her during one of those parties. They had left the ballroom and stood alone together on the terrace looking up at the glowing moon and the star-filled brilliance of the night. "I am a different man. I am a man who has fallen in love for the first time."

Eleanor beamed with pleasure. She felt empowered because of the happiness she was bringing him. So, she later told Charlotte. Brice was like the sleeping prince who has wakened to a new and glorious world that allows him to see his beloved and himself with soul-searching clarity.

When they returned to the ballroom, Alan observed them with the sting of suspicion and with a rising animosity.

Charlotte watched him, pleased that he was learning what it means to feel betrayed by the person to whom he had given so much of his love.

More than once, he struggled to explore with Charlotte the tremendous changes that were overtaking their marriage. Though he had not made love to Charlotte for many weeks, he still felt a deep-seated affection for her.

What he had lost in their relationship was his desire for her. He did not know whether he would ever recapture his sensual need of her. He wondered whether she would always be an essential part of his life. He wondered what his life might become if he were not intertwined with her, a brave woman who had withstood the horrors of war and whose battle-haunted presence recalled for him every day the death that surrounded them during those horrific four years. Without her, he could become a new man, somebody other than the soul-damaged man he was now and would always be if he remained partnered with her.

"Maybe we'd be happier apart," he told her. "Maybe we could forget the memories that bind us together."

Imagining a new life with Eleanor appealed to him. He would never lose his sexual need of Eleanor. He could not imagine life without her.

Charlotte listened to him with quiet patience. She pitied him, and she still loved him. She believed that she could help him find his way through the darkness.

"You want to escape the scenes of war that will not leave you," she said. "You want to be free of your anguish. But that is not possible. I don't know whether we will spend the rest of our lives remembering the horrors of the war. I do know that, if we can't forget those horrors, we need to go on living well in spite of them. Eleanor isn't the answer for you. She's merely a temporary fix. Brice is my occasional pleasure. We may want them to be part of our lives forever. But they won't stay. We won't be able to hold them back. They will soon go out of our lives. When they do, we will come back to each other. We will continue to make our lives an adventure."

Hearing all that she was telling him, Alan studied her with a penetrating gaze. He was impressed that his affair with Eleanor was not altering Charlotte's belief that theirs would be a lasting marriage. Nevertheless, he posed a question meant to challenge that belief.

"What if we don't come back to each other?"

The tough-minded part of her nature pushed Charlotte to answer him with no show of sentimentality or of trepidation.

"We'll bear up," she answered him. "We'll hurry on to the next adventures."

Only once did he mention Brice's coupling with Eleanor.

He mentioned Eleanor and Brice to her on an evening when they were getting dressed for one of the extravagant celebrations that always made Newport summers both glamorous and famous. Alan was wearing with masculine authority an off-white ivory linen suit, an azure silk shirt, a cobalt blue tie, and summer-white evening shoes. Charlotte's assurance and poise enhanced the beauty of her free-spirited ochre-colored floral dress and her ochre satin-beaded shoes. Together, they had the look of an ideal romantic couple. In this phase of their marriage, though, they both understood that they were neither romantic nor ideal.

At this precise moment, Alan allowed himself to frown. A darker thought was disturbing his usual equanimity. He threw out a question to Charlotte.

"What is happening between Eleanor and Brice?"

Seated at her ivory-gold French Provincial vanity and peering at her mirrored image, Charlotte offered him a casual reply as she applied the lightest gloss to her lips.

"They are having a good time."

"They are too often together."

"They are simply two young people enjoying the summer. When you are not around and Eleanor needs an escort, Brice becomes a convenient friend. Perhaps, eventually, he will become the only lover she needs."

Her words brought no comfort to Alan. Nor did the days that followed comfort him. It was during these days that Alan detected an even more noticeable change in Eleanor. She grew less attentive to their relationship and, while invoking careful subtleties, was finding excuses not to be in his company.

One time when they were alone together at a shooting range that spread outward from the swank interior of a Newport rifle-and-pistol club, she quietly offered him reasons why they could not often be together.

"My math and science studies take much of my time," she told him. "When I have some free time and you are not available, Charlotte always invites me to join her on various excursions. When I am alone with you, everything becomes right again. Life is especially good to us at least some of the time. Let's not ask for more than that."

Having said so, she lightly touched his lips with a kiss. Her blue eyes gleamed with happiness.

He returned the kiss with a passion that indicated he had made a serious claim for her love. His kiss also suggested that he was not willing to forsake that claim.

The long, firm press of his lips upon her lips disconcerted her and left her breathless.

When she found her breath once more, she tried to make light of his passion. She laughed a nervous laugh and with her soft hands delicately touched his face.

"You are so intense about everything," she said. "Too intense. You enjoy treating me as a possession. But that is not the way to my heart."

"It's the only way I can make the journey," he answered her. "It's the way I make my claim. It's my way of telling you I am not going to give up my claim."

He smiled after he had spoken these words. The smile softened the bluntness of his remark and its troubling implications.

She also smiled and kept a lilt in her voice.

"Find another way to my heart," she said. "That will be a new adventure for both of us."

Having said so, she carefully took hold of her Colt 1911 semi-automatic pistol that was known for its accuracy. With her dominant hand—her gun hand—she clasped the pistol high on the back of the grip. Doing so gave her more leverage against the weapon. It would help her to control the recoil when she fired it. She placed her support hand so that it pressed firmly against the exposed portion of the grip not covered by her gun hand. As she did so, she was placing all four fingers of her hand under the trigger guard and pressing her index finger hard underneath it. She stood with her feet and hips shoulder-width apart. She bent her knees slightly so that she could fire the pistol with stability as well as with mobility. She raised the Colt toward the H-shaped steel target stand and toward as well the heavy paper target that stood within it a hundred yards away. It had a bullseye in its center and an underlying one-inch grid. She pressed the trigger straight to the rear and increased the pressure. She fired her pistol. She hit the target.

"You are improving," Alan said. "You are getting better and better."

Eleanor answered him with teasing words.

"Not only on a pistol range," she said.

"I know," he said. "I know it very well."

After that day at the pistol range, his need for Eleanor grew even more intense. In her absence, his bitterness deepened. The thought that Brice had displaced him intensified his anger.

Charlotte enjoyed observing Alan's discomfort. But, at the same time, she was aware with awakened clarity that Alan's discomfort might anchor itself not only to dismay and regret, but also to danger and revenge.

CHAPTER TEN
WARNINGS

Alan began studying Eleanor's daily activities with proprietary furtiveness. Wily and accurate, he examined the subtexts and implications of their relationship. Recalling all the times that they were together, he analyzed the realism of his belief that she belonged to him and that she was going to be his life partner.

Now in the second week of August, three months had passed since he and Charlotte brought their unorthodox influences into her life. It was seven weeks ago—the twentieth of June—when he began sleeping with Eleanor. With Charlotte as her guardian tutor, Eleanor was learning to choose and to appreciate the gifts which her status as Gerald Marnham's granddaughter kept offering her. She was also learning to fulfill all the obligations that her acceptance of those gifts, in good conscience and with fair-minded reciprocity, entailed.

The varied scenes that brought them together came swiftly back to him while he pondered their influences upon Eleanor and upon himself.

He was aware that communicating the whole day

long with remarkable Charlotte in French or Italian, German or Danish or Spanish brought Eleanor a special pleasure. She found equal pleasure in speaking to him occasionally in French, Italian, and German. He was aware, as she was, that each day not only intensified her disciplined aptitudes, but also prepared her for a life in the wider world. Partnered with him, she would find that experience even more adventurous and more creative than the everyday reality which now spun its ambivalence around her. He had to move with caution. He had to wait for the precisely right moment. It was always going to be challenging and sometimes surprising to collaborate with her soft loveliness. Wily and astute, he planned to accompany her to a further discovery of her immense and untested possibilities. He wanted to be one with her. He wanted to be the co-creator of her reborn self and the ingenious shaper of her destiny.

So it was, in the full consciousness of her evolution and with worldly-wise and war-ravaged Charlotte and him as her toughminded mentors, that in these swiftly passing months Eleanor was learning from each day's challenging studies and altruistic endeavors the virtues of maintaining an intellectual rigor toward herself, especially in tense or formidable circumstances. She was also learning the virtues of helping those who are poor or sick or abandoned in old age to a lonely dying. At the same time, she was guiding to a better path young hollow men who were incorrigible failures, promiscuous drug-addicted females still in their teens, and ex-convicts of both genders.

Though his sympathies did not always extend to these self-defeating losers, he pushed himself forward as a dedicated reformer—an empathetic man who wanted to help these downtrodden people—these abject failures—to save themselves. It was not in his hardened character to extend his hand to moral weaklings and burnt-out wretches. But he made every effort. He did all that he could do. He set an example without in any profound or personal way validating its meaningfulness for his own life or registering a claim to the authenticity of his public service. He altered the scenario. He revised the plan in which Charlotte alone would inspire Eleanor to enlarge her capacities for achieving her worthiest aspirations. His influence, paradoxically both liberal and appropriating, worked its ambiguous powers upon her. After the first weeks of their meeting as teacher and pupil, Eleanor and he quickly achieved a natural rapport as passionate lovers. Their need for one another became a pressing desire and a furious ecstasy. Apart from their frequent copulation, he became for her a gentle advisor and a discreet mentor. Not only did he draw from her a flawless performance as a student of calculus, trigonometry, biology, and architectural engineering. He also accompanied her, with intellectually solid Charlotte as his associate, through advanced programs in the history of world cultures.

More than that, in these months with Charlotte as Eleanor's primary guide and with him as an earnest participant in their worthwhile endeavors, there occurred during the many Samaritan visits they paid to the sick or poor, as well as to the aged or injured, the clearest evidence of Eleanor's progress away from the sometimes impulsive and often self-absorbed girl her privileged background had influenced her to be. Though these gestures of charity altered none of Charlotte's or his cynical view of humanity and of the world in which their fallible species exists, these visits to the downtrodden awakened Eleanor's compassion for those human beings who were far less fortunate than she was. On these beneficent visits to the needy and in the presence of Charlotte's authentic empathy toward the suffering and the needy and his artful simulation of such empathy, Eleanor had acquitted herself effectively. With the quietude of a humble nurse, she had administered the corporal works of mercy that had brought her to the working-class suburbs which stood, unobtrusive and ordinary, beyond the visible rims of Newport. Never before had she completely entered the experience of sharing her humanness with these struggling members of her species who often, despite their hardships, maintained a proud and undaunted resilience.

That Eleanor was beginning to explore a similar resilience impressed him. During these later Samaritan visits of this first season of her recovery, she was discovering within herself a profound sympathy for the anguished and afflicted and abandoned. There grew in her a genuine desire to do all that she could to help them. In this period, she often brought her solacing presence to girls and boys dying from heart ailments or from brain tumors. The stoic resignation of these children—no more than seven or eight years old—intensified their quiet acceptance of their fates. On other days he witnessed Eleanor prodding a young, embittered war hero toward new self-determination as he was learning to walk again, assisted as he was by a prosthetic leg. So moved was she by his plight, that she persuaded her uncle to finance his enrollment into law school. When this young hero earned his law degree, there would be a place for him within the legal department of the Marnham Steel Corporation. In the weeks that followed and when he could pull himself away from the building commissions and the exemplary staff that Gerald had given him, he—with convincing benevolent energies—helped Eleanor and Charlotte and their team of able assistants to paint and to furnish three large brownstones, so that the children and the widows of firefighters and policemen killed in the line of duty could make comfortable homes in attractive, modern apartments. To these afflicted human beings and to others like them, enlightened Eleanor, pragmatic Charlotte, and he—earthbound Alan Aubray— offered the sustenance of food and clothing and empathetic words.

There were, at this time, many other frail or fallible persons and a few derelicts and former drug addicts whose spirits revived because of Eleanor's presence. As if each time were a revelation meant for her alone, there came upon her awareness the truth that each of these suffering and broken and needy belonged to herself. They belonged, that is, to the human family she represented. So Charlotte had told him about these visits. So, also, he sometimes witnessed. Eleanor's new knowledge and the clarity of accurate recognition taught her to receive these suffering and broken and needy human beings, in the very hour she was assisting them, as upright and worthy relations.

In the quickened days of this summer, both Charlotte and he were surprised and very pleased by Eleanor's spontaneous expressions of sympathy and by the efficacy of her Samaritan deeds. He began to believe that this rigorous period of displacing her grief was making Eleanor a most capable human being. He was not surprised that he had so quickly fallen in love with her. With wakened clarity, he became aware of his love for her in an unexpected way. On one of her blue days, a question that Eleanor tearfully imparted enfolded his new awareness of her precious existence and his need to make her his life's partner. He wanted the adventure that he called his own life to enfold her for all the earthbound years that time might dispense to them and for all eternity.

"Is it so wrong to want life?" she had asked him.

He could not recall whether Charlotte was present.

Eleanor was challenging him to gainsay the rightness of her inquiry. But, quickly noticing his courteous reticence, she hurried on to express the vibrant idea that gave to the timbre of her voice a harder edge and a tough-minded urgency.

"I want only life."

"And I shall be a part of it," he gently promised.

His enthusiasm rose discreetly at the prospect of rescuing this appealing, vulnerable young woman. For he saw in that rescue a worthy calling for himself. A proper care and a profound love could infuse his days with a profounder meaning that might sometimes surprise, if not altogether startle, him.

"I'll show you the way back to happiness," he reassured her, as though happiness were for Eleanor and for him a recovered possibility—and a bit of wild luck and blessed chance.

"There will be days and days of happiness for you," he told her. His husky timbres ignited friendly capacities and whatever other guardian powers he possessed for dispelling a haunted girl's grief.

And so there were hours and days and weeks of happiness to revive at first and then enthrall her. So many times, sometimes with Charlotte and often alone, he drew her into festive occasions that flashed with quick time's waves and ripples. In the beginning, he took care always to guide her to the wholesome peers her family had in previous summers allowed her to befriend—hardy, keen-minded youths full-grown now and well-bred ethereal girls. Afterwards, when he chose to be alone with her, they sailed across the light of the sun welling beneath the tinted sea. With her, he swam with acrobatic glee, all swift and gleaming spume-flecked motion. Without the spate of life-loving friends (her trustworthy chums, along with Gerald's proven-loyal circle) that he regarded as intrusive, they—he and Eleanor—entered the colored velocity of a county fair. As an agreeable companion in that summer of surprises, he dared her with him beside her to climb her way to a perilous ridge. Just beyond a spotted raven's nest and twisted knots of grass, she—with him ascending adroitly—saw and heard, as for the first time because so proximate and actual, the rapid wingbeat of a black-backed gull. There, on that same ridge, they also observed the iridescent curve of cloud-flame cresting the hill above them and for one astonishing moment understood, as well, the symmetry and slant of the floating sky.

Through all these bracing occasions he restored Eleanor's capacities for claiming the extraordinary possibility that was her young life unfolding. Yet, at first, he could dispel only occasionally the quiet sorrow that sometimes and always with tensile aptitudes stole the glowing light from her eyes. As if in spite of an hour's chance happiness, her sorrow revealed itself steadfast and intrinsic, like a palpable substance that was slowly burning away her soul.

Still, there grew around her, around this lost, lovely young woman who with his guardian powers assisting might after all be wonderfully rescued, hours and days and weeks that possessed the very spirit and pleasure by which she herself yearned to be possessed. Flourishing and supreme, here-and-now experience rose upon her senses and was so much more intensified than any mind-held happiness that from her hovering past could only be a remembered idea. Or so he at that time told himself after she consented to explore with him unexpected occasions and secretly arranged meetings. Joining with him in the full fervor of summer moments, the two of them hurried together into a brave exhilaration. Then she knew a sweep of liberty whose startling rush and lift and emphasis were realistic measures of how much of her bright promise he was capable of saving.

His recollection of these astonishing scenes enabled

him to comprehend with new clarity her importance in his life. They also convinced him that he must never allow her to leave him.

That there was so much brightness to save, he perceived with casual-seeming attentiveness whenever Eleanor gave herself completely to the day's adventure. Observing her luminous form ascending a sun-glanced hill or riding the crest of wind-sheared waves or taming the curve of a billowing sail, he saw how fluently, given her will, her identity translated its differences. On those days she was for him and for others with a mind to notice as a lovely blossoming of nature, a flowering of crisp intention and act and emotion. The various meanings of herself became distilled through an array of nuances and emblems and increments that refused to be brought within the rule of arbitrary definition or any other narrowness.

Too often, though, there lingered, as if fastened about the tense capacities of her sorrow, a guilty reluctance to bring her own fervor to the festive weeks that he—without Charlotte—was providing. Each day now he regarded as a favorable sign of her wakening spirit every occasion when Eleanor, as if suddenly confident and self-governing, willed herself effortlessly to explore with him a day that made happiness seem, if not permanent, at least diverse and plausible. For that reason, he was heartened whenever she offered herself to the day's unexpected flare of surprise and to the promise, as well, of wildness not unlike adventure. This willowy image of nearly blithe Eleanor brought him a quiet pleasure. For she appeared in those moments to be recovering all the happiness that she felt had been taken from her. What quickened his heartbeat was something even more essential to the plans that he was making for the both of them together. She was falling in love with him. So he told himself, roused whenever he looked upon her wind-tanned oval face, blonde hair, and clipped, New England voice that enhanced her quiet confidence and crisp directness.

After he initiated his affair with her, he looked back upon the many weeks when he had rarely been alone with her and had held himself to rigorous discipline as perverse masochism and self-defeating asceticism. He did not need to be alone to share with her the furtive glances and to savor the pleasures of dancing, as if casually, with her at the grand parties that her grandfather hosted on so many Newport summer days. The guests, as young as he was and older, accepted his guardian regard of her as a natural reflection of his strong bond with her grandfather and of his careful breeding, yoked as his conduct was to a reserved demeanor and to well-modulated propriety. He was not alone with her when, in mid-June, they played tennis with Gerald and Sylvia or when, a day after that, he water-skied beside her across the wide span of sun-tinted Saranac Lake in upstate

New York. That time, he and Charlotte were spending a weekend at a luxurious French-style chalet with Gerald, Sylvia, and Eleanor and with several of Gerald's business friends and their wives.

Nor was he alone with her when, during the fourth-of-July holiday, they swam in the heated pool within the south wing of her grandfather's Newport home or when, during that same week, they rode their Arab bays on a horse farm in Camden, Maine. Yet, on every occasion, whether he was seated next to her at a dinner table or guiding her through a waltz or conversing with her at the bar of a supper club or standing beside her in front of an Impressionist canvas in an art gallery, he conveyed through the press of his hand upon her shoulder or through the sensual implications of his husky voice or through his seductive glances the passion that was stirring within him. Because of the canny instincts that he had cultivated by means of his realistic negotiations with the world, he kept his passion a secret to everyone except Eleanor and Charlotte.

In the first moments after he opened his heart to her in mid-June, she recognized the poignancy in his ardor. She noticed, too, the care he took to conceal his feelings from everybody except her. His secrecy was a device for protecting her reputation and for avoiding public declarations of his love that could throw the two of them, as well as her grandfather, into turmoil. Yet he was no callow youth. From the time he was eighteen, he was a man of the world. Privileged, artistic, and ambitious in the years when he was a student in the École Polytechnique in Paris, he had engaged in exciting liaisons with a film starlet, with a nightclub chanteuse, and with the equally promiscuous girls who were his age and who belonged to his social class. A vigorous university man in those happy days before the war, he was testing his prowess with all those women in sexual encounters that were, to him, satisfying biological acts that involved no profound emotions and no commitment beyond an hour's sensation in an upscale hotel or in a private ski lodge or in a well-appointed cabin on a pristine yacht.

But his feelings for Eleanor were altogether different. Though he had loved Charlotte with life-affirming passion through all the dark days of the war, they needed to walk away from each other. Their battle-scarred souls would never allow them to find happiness while they lived together. He needed someone new who could help him resurrect the hopeful and idealistic young man that the war had killed—the Alan Aubray who could make life spin faster and faster, the daring engineer who found adventure in the new, the passionate man who could take possession of a lost girl and teach her to become his loyal and adventurous woman.

After his penetrating eyes looked back upon the scenes that he and Eleanor had shared and after his quickened mind evaluated the sum and substance of their meaning for his relationship with her, Alan felt even more convinced that he and Eleanor belonged together. Yet there lingered within his awareness the next step he needed to take if he were to arrive at the incontrovertible truth that the happier Fates or an exciting destiny or blind chance had all along been quietly intertwining Eleanor's life with his own. The next step involved his confronting Eleanor with his new message of undying love and his urgent request that she reveal—without murmured hesitation or limiting conditions of any kind—the whole truth of her feelings for him.

All during the following weekend, which wore festive colors and summertime exuberance inside one of Gerald's parties, he noticed that beneath Eleanor's glamorous appearance there lived—as though it were a will-o'-the-wisp image that revealed its nature only in temporary flashes—a sadness that melded itself to both guilt and remorse.

It was this same image that he noticed upon finding Eleanor standing pensive and solitary at the blue-rimmed well in Gerald's rose garden. All about her were the harmonies of floribunda and hybrid teas, delicate rosemary and damask and blue-moon surfaces. Cloistered there, within the shadows of late afternoon, Eleanor appeared tentative and melancholic. Not even the orange, yellow, and white splendor of rhododendrons and the red, lavender, and cream petals of camellias could dissuade her from her sorrow. Nor, he imagined, could the golden-yellow leaves and glossy, rounded red fruits of the pomegranate tree ease her troubled awareness that the confident young woman—her reborn self—that she had discovered in the earlier summer weeks had now become, to herself if not to others, an uncertain stranger.

During the unfolding of the splendid party, he had noticed her mingling with many of the guests. He had also noticed that she permitted herself to dance only with Brice. Her discreet withdrawal from the party had not yet roused the attention of the guests or even of Brice. But he—Alan Aubray, the man who did not care to exist without her— had noticed. His gaze upon her, furtive and angry, held her always within the parameters of his conflicted attention. When he saw her taking leave of the party and hurrying into the garden, he quickly followed her. No sooner had he reached the threshold of the garden, than he caught sight of her in the dusk-laden distance that separated them. She was standing by the blue-rimmed well, lost in sullenness and recrimination. Rather than intrude upon her too abruptly, he spoke to her with clear-voiced affability while he stood a few steps beyond the ornate French doors that opened to the garden.

"The guests will start missing you," he said. "You are the princess of this party. Everyone wants to make a friend of you."

She turned to face him, but she did not answer him at once. She considered the friendly timbre of his voice and the courtesy of his staying apart from her at least in this moment. Only after that did she bring a smile to her lips. Only then did she allow her eyes to glow because he and nobody else was standing there carefully observing her. After that, she imparted cordial words that pushed back though they did not conceal her melancholy.

"Even a princess needs to stand alone sometime," she said, "especially when she can stand alone in a luxurious garden away from the excitement of a party."

"Is that what you want?" he asked, still keeping his place by the door. "You want to stand alone?"

"Not now," she answered him. "Not now, when you are here."

She kept her smile and beckoned him forward.

Together, they took their places on a comfortable bench not far from the topiaries of a doe and her fawn. For a few minutes, they sat together without uttering a word. To a casual observer, they might have appeared as a romantic couple who had come to the garden to breathe the crisp air and to savor the variety of colors that, in their scanning glances, wore the fleet emphases of a montage or the imagery within a kaleidoscope. Before their contemplative eyes, the oncoming night was changing the colors of flowers and ferns and of trees and shrubs, disguising in subtle ways the reality of their forms. A soft wind with tactile energies was animating these forms even as the fading light kept translating them into eerie and watchful presences.

Or so Alan allowed himself to muse, for that moment regarding the imagery around Eleanor and him as an ambiguous play upon his senses. Only after that did he turn to observe Eleanor as she sat beside him, taut within an interior stillness that held her to its steadfast ordinances. Sorrow worked as a shadow upon her elegant beauty, redefining the intricacies of her poise and of her pensive manner. Usually austere in his responses, he was moved by the nearly imperceptible hint of anguish that she was struggling to keep at bay. His unease at witnessing that struggle pushed him forward while he dispelled the silence that had momentarily held them in its powers.

"I've been noticing how unhappy you are," he said. "Maybe you would like to tell me why. Sometimes it's good to bring these secrets into the open."

At first, Eleanor remained silent. Very carefully, she was studying his face and, at the same time, weighing the consequences of telling him the cause of her sorrow.

Alan nudged her forward.

"Go ahead," he said. "Tell me all of it. The truth won't break me apart. Nor should you allow it to break you."

His words reassured her. Now she was willing to tell him the cause of her sorrow.

"It's you," she said. "Tonight, I can't be completely happy because I know that I have to make you unhappy. I have to tell you that we can no longer be lovers. I've fallen in love with Brice. There is no room in my heart for any other man. I'm going to be faithful to him for the rest of my life."

Alan felt a fierce anger rising inside him. Only his stern willfulness held back its fury. Only his inveterate wiliness harnessed its danger. He chose temperate words to tell what he was feeling.

"Brice can never love you as I do—completely and passionately and unconditionally. With you beside me, I am somebody new. I have recovered the happiness that the war had stolen from me. You have not only given me your love. You have resurrected me from the dead."

A frown creased Eleanor's brow. A pleading look touched her face for just an instant and just as quickly vanished.

"You have to let me go," Eleanor said. Her voice was matter of fact now. She was not petitioning him. She was offering him the good counsel he needed to hear. "You have to rediscover your love for Charlotte."

He quickly resisted her counsel.

"I'm not in love with Charlotte," he said. "I'm in love with you."

"Falling in love with each other was never part of our agreement," Eleanor reminded him. "Of course, I love you for all the wonderful things that we have shared. But I am not *in love* with you. Fall in love with Charlotte again. She needs your love, and I believe that you need hers."

Still he resisted her words.

"Charlotte doesn't need me. She's a survivor. She'll find her way to another man."

Eleanor told him more. She chose the words that he did not want to hear.

"I've found the man I plan to live with forever. I've found Brice. We've found each other. We are going to be married next month."

He grew very still, as though he needed the stillness to decipher the meanings of her blunt words. When he answered her, he brought new conviction to his words. He wanted to sound reasonable. He was serving her a warning. "Your grandfather will never allow the marriage. Brice's reputation has preceded him even here in Newport. He's been an ardent lover for plenty of women. But he's never allowed himself to fall in love with any of them. You need to take care. Don't throw yourself into danger."

Eleanor challenged his words. She resisted his warning.

"Brice has fallen in love with me, and I have fallen in love with him."

Eleanor rose from her place on the bench. She looked once more about her. Darkness was falling around them, concealing trees and shrubs as well as flowers and foliage. Only the pale moon permitted them to see—as discolored fragments or ellipses—the summer splendor of the garden.

Alan, too, left his place on the bench and joined her as they moved toward the French doors that would enable them to reenter the ballroom where the lavish party was still in full swing. The orchestra was playing a new set of love ballads while well-preserved women in floral gowns and well-groomed men in light-weight tuxedos were dancing with casual poise. Uninhibited laughter and merry voices also rose across the ballroom while other guests were dining and conversing at banquet tables or drinking at the bar. Alan appraised the scene with cynical eyes. Just before he guided Eleanor back to the table where Gerald, Sylvia, and Brice as well as many of her friends were waiting for her return, he had something important to tell her. His words were as terse as they were direct.

"If you marry Brice, you will be killing me," he said. "I can no longer live without you."

"You will bear up," she said. "You survived the war. You will survive our relationship."

Once again, he served her his warning.

"I tell you that you will be killing me. You will be killing the happiness that belongs to both of us."

She did not use new words to respond to his warning. Instead, she moved ahead of him, quietly eclipsing the impression that they were entering the ballroom together.

When she reached the banquet table where the people who loved her were waiting, she brought genuine elation to the greeting she offered them.

Her grandfather and Sylvia, as well as Brice and their friends, were delighted that she had returned with such beaming vitality. They offered her warm-hearted greetings and approving smiles.

"I couldn't stay away a moment longer," she assured them. "I've missed all of you so very much."

Brice rose from his place and offered her his hand as he guided her to a seat next to him.

"Did you really miss us that much?" he asked her with teasing emphasis. He was waiting for her to say the special words that would bring him even more pleasure.

She read his mind well. She understood the yearning in his heart.

"Of course, I did," she answered him. "In fact, I

missed *you* most of all."

Finding his place next to Charlotte, Alan observed them—Eleanor and Brice—with suppressed animosity and a concealed resolve to destroy their relationship.

The next afternoon, his determination to keep Eleanor for himself alone pushed him to win Gerald's favor in this matter of Eleanor's romance with Brice. He had been conferring with Gerald in that ambitious man's study about the progress that he and his team were making to bring modern textures to his Newport property without sacrificing its classic ambiance.

In this specific moment of their meeting, just after they had concluded their discussion about the work that his team of architects and civil engineers had already accomplished, Gerald was seated, implacable and straight-backed, at his desk. As in previous meetings here, Alan admired the desk. The nineteenth-century bow-fronted mahogany pedestal partnered handsomely with a green leather top. The round brass pulls on its drawers embellished a distinctive aesthetic.

While maintaining the requirements of his own canny equilibrium, he was seated within the familiar comfort of a Carlyle chair. Its generously padded, button-tufted back and fixed seat cushion were an Edwardian abundance, as were the serene-rich hues in stripes of beige and gold and navy. The chair's maple legs on brass casters enhanced a correct and amplified solidity.

During this carefully modulated encounter, he recognized once again the balance and proportion and intricate clarity of this special room of Gerald's.

Here and now, in this latest visit to the study, he noticed the splendid design of the room and the implicated meanings within that design. He and Charlotte had sometimes discussed this room and the ways that it effectively became a metaphoric continuation of the exterior life unfolding around and upon Gerald's property. On the high-ceilinged, pale-yellow wall behind and above the desk where Gerald sat, the vivid splendors of Monet's *Regattas at Argenteuil* complemented and intensified the summer day's grand propensities—all the excited imagery informing the expansive arched windows that opened to a garden and to the sea nearby.

That imagery offered to his glance as he faced Gerald and faced, as well, the windows' sumptuous prospect beyond and to the right of him, colorful sailboats that rose upon his seeing like bright flares in the distance hurrying across cerulean, sun-mottled waters. Mastering its own ascension, inhabiting as it did the wall directly behind and above Gerald's desk in vaulted, cathedral space, the extraordinary *Regattas* with correspondent powers also vitalized the spacious circumference of a discriminating man's study. Surely, on this canvas Monet not only emulated Nature's implicated harmonies. He also taught the spectator visiting it how, more authentically, to see.

Subtly and deftly, Monet teaches us to see. So, Charlotte and he had agreed right after their first meeting with Gerald on the tenth of May. Now, on the twelfth of August and in keen attentiveness, Alan was about to affirm his wish to be for Eleanor Farrell the auspicious influence the girl needed if she was to be rescued from a precipitate marriage to Brice Fontaine. Before he imparted that sentiment to Gerald, he reviewed the information that the room was revealing about its owner.

Braced by new perceiving (he told himself), we accept the aggregate of blotches in the lower part of Monet's canvas as gestures of paint translating colored ripples on the water. Broad, italic strokes clarify the painter's act even as they reflect and guide us to the upper part of the canvas and the instantly discernible reality of amber-luminous sailboats, cobalt-green hedges and trees, and houses wearing emphatic red roofs beneath an understated azure sky.

Still the bright flares that were sailboats flourished within sight of Gerald's property and upon his scanning glance toward the arched windows of this study before which he sat. Still their kinetic, sailing rhythms went on hurrying across sun-mottled Newport waters in the cerulean distance.

There was, he had agreed with Charlotte, something happily artful about this juxtaposition of Monet's canvas on the wall behind and above Gerald's desk and of the Newport seascape quickening the prospect beyond the windows of his study. This melding of literal and metaphoric and of outside world and inner reflected the balance and coherence of the life that Gerald Marnham invited to unfold around him. It was this disciplined symmetry and its scrupulously designed perfection which (Alan imagined) Gerald sought as the most meaningful pattern of life—his life in particular and the lives of his son Austin, who was married and who was striving to make at least some of his own life's choices while working within his father's corporation in Pittsburgh, and his granddaughter Eleanor, who—while gradually recovering from the tragic loss of her parents—was becoming a young woman both self-assured and adventurous.

Yet, Monet's complicity with Nature located the spontaneous in energetic daring. His peerless seeing was an extemporary gesture, or it seemed so. There was little of that art in Gerald's engagement with reality. In fact, there was very little of that liberality we call instinct or intuition and, sometimes, adventure. For Monet (and, yes, for Charlotte and him and Eleanor, too—they had the same spirit) all of life was an astonishing kaleidoscope. It was a veritable stereopticon inviting each of us to define our own arts through its many colors. But Gerald, though an immensely successful corporate leader, did not seek the full spectrum of life. It was not his way to experience the manifold colors of life or to test their vibrancies and hidden values. Instead, he worked from the subdued palette which hesitates to identify its proficiencies through unconstrained gesture or willful experiment or impulsive daring.

So Alan and Charlotte had believed, even in their first meeting with Gerald three months earlier. During that first meeting and from his casual remarks about his relations with the daughter who had died and with a son who strove to fulfill his father's will, they—Alan and Charlotte—were aware that Gerald had become inflexible in his prescriptions for the well-being of his offspring. Even while experiencing a subdued dismay at his paternal arbitrariness, though, they respected him for heeding the voice of his own conscience. Yet that respect and admiration had not kept them from quietly invoking a more realistic program concerning Eleanor's future.

Now, in mid-August, Alan had taken a seat here in this study because he wanted to persuade Gerald against Eleanor's marrying Brice. Gerald noticed the tension within him, but he did not push him forward. Instead, he waited politely for him to find the words that would explain his unease.

Recognizing his moment, Alan did find the words

that identified him as the teacherly advocate of Eleanor's happiness.

"I am worried about Eleanor," he began. "She talks of marrying Brice. But she can't really be in love with him. Her feelings for him are merely a schoolgirl's infatuation for a young man who has led a wild and adventurous life. She will never find lasting happiness with him."

After hearing his impassioned words, Gerald remained silent for a few moments. With studious awareness, he observed Alan's genuine concern that Eleanor might be choosing as her life's partner a young man who would bring her to grief. Only after taking the full measure of Alan's dismay did Gerald say the words that to his mind were both pertinent and appropriate.

"You want to protect Eleanor's interests," he said. "You regard her as your sister. Your attitude toward her is most commendable. But you need not worry. Everything is working itself out. In fact, it couldn't be better."

His words surprised Alan, who needed to know what they meant.

"But her relationship to Brice—there's danger in it."

"I understand your concern," Gerald said. "You want to keep Eleanor safe from harm and from wrong choices that will bring her to grief. That's all to the good and speaks well of your character. But you need not worry. In fact, this is a time for celebration. Eleanor *is* going to marry

Brice—and very soon. They will be married next month. The merging of Marnham and Fontaine blood is the best news I've heard in a long time."

"What about Eleanor's schooling? I thought that she planned to attend Bryn Mawr next year."

"Bryn Mawr will not be in her future. There is every reason to believe that, a year from now, she will pass examinations that will allow her to enter Radcliffe College as a sophomore. When that time arrives, she and Brice will live in a luxurious townhouse not far from Harvard. Within the next week or so, she has a very good chance of passing, as well, the special entrance examinations to the Sorbonne. Brice, still connected to Harvard, will complete his third year of study in Paris at the École Polytechnique. Eleanor and Brice will spend their first year of marriage studying in Paris. That is as romantic as a year's study can get."

"Are you certain that Eleanor is doing the right thing?"

"Of course, I am. They are going to have a very happy life together."

"I am pleased you believe that," Alan said. "I'll try to believe it, too."

"Of course, you will. And so will Charlotte. I know that both of you want what is best for Eleanor."

"That's the very thing," Alan said. "We want what is best for her."

Gerald was smiling as they ended their conference.

Alan also smiled, as though he were in complete accord with Gerald's point of view.

But he was not pleased.

What was best for Eleanor involved *him*, not Brice.

He spent long hours of the next days working assiduously with his team to activate further his ambitious plans for Gerald's property. The work exhausted him at the same time that it lifted his spirit. At night, though, his brooding returned—furtive and dangerous. He spent these nights away from Eleanor and away even from Charlotte, though he and Charlotte continued to share adjoining bedrooms. That they slept in separate rooms did not attract undue notice, because he often worked late into the night at a drafting table in his bedroom. His allowing Charlotte to maintain her own privacy was proof of his respect for her and his deference.

Away from Charlotte and from Eleanor, he brooded in the bitter quiet of his aloneness. He felt trapped inside a darkness whose depths he had not yet plumbed. His losing Eleanor would, he believed, drive him into the madness from which there is no return. Already, in these few days when she remained absent from his life, he felt as though he were suffocating. He found breathing difficult. The panic attacks that he had eluded during the war when, with bayoneted rifle in hand, he was rushing toward enemies across muddy battlefields strewn with the shattered and disfigured bodies of young soldiers, began now to overtake him in the wretched solitude of his nights. He tossed and turned and only sporadically fell into the anguished uneasiness of sleep.

He began to have a recurring nightmare. Caught inside its violent implications, he was wreaking vengeance against Brice Fontaine, the wily adversary who had stolen Eleanor away from him. Night after night, this recurring dream ignited his hatred of Brice and his fury.

In this nightmare, he and Brice were hunting red deer in a forest in Maine. Dark clouds were menacing the October sky and rendering the pale-yellow sun spectral and ominous. Strong winds were tossing awry the branches of leaning, vulnerable trees. Lightning flashed and scarred the air and scooped away bronze-colored leaves and russet-colored bushes. Birds with large beaks clustered in tall trees, and tawny foxes scampered inside murky corners of the forest. Undeterred by the gathering storm, he and Brice continued to pursue the red deer. Sighting it in the distance at the top of a dark green hill, Brice wielded his Winchester with masterly control, took steady aim, and with well-honed accuracy, shot and killed the stag. As he hurried forward to claim his prize, Alan called to him. When, at the crest of the hill, Brice turned to face him, Alan raised his rifle and, with lethal marksmanship, fired a bullet into Brice's forehead. Brice's body dropped across the body of the dead stag, lingered there momentarily, and then fell as if flung down the long, winding hill.

The shock of this nightmare and its surreal nature pushed Alan awake. Startled and wary, he recalled every action in his nightmare. Its sinister nature disturbed him as much as his continuing recollection of the battlefields and the killings into which the recent war had plunged him. Alone now in the moonlit darkness of his solitary bedroom, he took several drags on a cigarette, deciphering the meaning of the recurring nightmare and accepting it as a warning. He leaned against his pillows and listened to the busy roar of ocean waves that rose upon the summer air and bonded with the quickened breeze that tapped like a frightened living creature against the panoramic window that overlooked his bedroom. Drained of his fury, he was nevertheless apprehensive that he might, in fact, kill Brice. Upon being discovered, he would spend the rest of his life in prison—away from the love of his life, away from Eleanor, without whom he did not care to go on living.

No, he would not kill Brice, even though he had grown to hate him. He had to choose a different path out of his dilemma. He had to find a path out of his nightmare that would unite him with Eleanor forever.

CHAPTER ELEVEN
THE PRICE OF HAPPINESS

In these busy weeks of August, Alan watched Eleanor's every move. Most of the time, he watched her from a distance. With an iron will that he had often made his ally, he resisted any outward show of interest in Eleanor whenever he chanced to be in the same room with her. Always, he made certain that other persons were also in those rooms that included Gerald's pristine study and the luxurious country club ballroom where Gerald and his friends often celebrated the lift and swing of summer evenings. At times, he found a natural place near Eleanor in the open, sun-dazzling spaces that included Gerald's private beach that looked upon the billowy waves of the ocean and that influenced the genuine exhilaration of friends her own age. The sun-dazzling spaces also influenced the fully declared happiness of Brice, Eleanor, Sylvia, and Gerald and the simulated happiness of Charlotte and their many Newport friends. On more than one occasion, while riding a swift, gold-coated palomino, he joined Eleanor, Brice, and Charlotte along the winding horse trail that hastened through paths that were bordered by giant elm trees and a rushing stream and that offered to his quickened glance scampering foxes, galloping deer, and flourishing russet bushes. During all of these occasions, he took special care to appear affable, easy-going, and contented.

At glamorous dinner dances, he offered amusing anecdotes and accorded those persons in his company respectful attention and subtly modulated camaraderie. He danced with Charlotte and Sylvia and with many other summertime ladies. But he did not dance with Eleanor, nor did she miss his presence because she had eyes only for Brice.

On a few afternoons atop the sun-burnished ocean waves that unfurled their energies along the beachfront of Gerald's property or in the cool waters of the scintillant pool that was located in the southwest wing that looked out upon the ocean, he swam with athletic supremacy and with the sheer joy that he managed to capture for an hour or two. He swam most often next to Charlotte and sometimes near Sylvia and Gerald. Occasionally, he swam next to country club couples, and one time near Brice and Eleanor. Always, he maintained his equanimity. Always, he acted as though he was a very happy man—a man who was comfortable in his own skin and who made others feel comfortable because of the pleasure they found in looking upon his freewheeling negotiations with joy.

During these busy and crowded days, he worked assiduously with his team of architects and civil and mechanical engineers to complete a major part of the work that was bringing a balanced modernity to Gerald's stately property. Among those skillful people was Brice Fontaine, whose work ethic and competent abilities made him an essential part of the team. Alan always found reason to praise his worthy efforts, even as he praised the effective work of other team members who had given evidence of their ingenuity, diligence, and originality. But his hatred of Brice festered secretly within his soul. Brice was his rival for the love of Eleanor, the only woman who could make him happy.

In the meantime, Charlotte and Eleanor attended summer lectures in mathematics, science, and literature within Brown University. Together, they continued their charitable works in the impoverished districts within Providence. They made Samaritan visits to the sick and the elderly in Newport and Middletown. With the assistance of expert horsemen, they taught elementary school children and a few middle school pupils how to ride a pony or a stallion. Within a wind-flowing meadow of wild grasses and upon colorful canvases supported by artists' easels, five girls and five boys—all of them from deprived backgrounds—were bringing to painterly life the images of sky and clouds and ocean, as well as sailboats and seagulls and a faraway lighthouse. The children's success at capturing the various truths of the scene, translated as those truths were through each child's original seeing, brought great pleasure to Charlotte and Eleanor, who were the teachers who inspired their best efforts.

So, Alan had observed on an afternoon when he and two members of his team were reviewing the ways that the main house claimed its own expressive individuality. It was located not at the water's edge, but farther back into the land, gaining thereby elevation and foreground and prospect. Yet the new configuration they had constructed neither neglected nor compromised Gerald's desire to be near the ocean. A swimming pool and pool house and pergola, emblematic of the human will activating its own propensities, now stood near and above the water's edge. The luster of the main house's ocean perch enhanced and imbued the presence of the swimming pool, the pool house, and the pergola.

His team's success in translating Gerald's wishes into reality gave Alan much satisfaction. His work as a landscape architect and as an engineer and the work of his team would live on for many years after he and his team had lived out their time here on earth. This achievement gave authentic meaning to his having survived the war. His restoration of Gerald's property had given his life purpose. He was pleased that in a day or two he would finish a major part of his work here.

On the fourteenth of August, Gerald and Sylvia initiated their plan to host a lavish dinner dance that, on Labor Day weekend, would celebrate the wedding of Eleanor and Brice. Renowned caterers, talented interior decorators, and accomplished musicians were already at work to make the evening extraordinary. Eleanor, Charlotte, and Sylvia had conferred with a New York couturier, who planned to create elegant gowns for Eleanor and her bridesmaids, as well as for Charlotte and Sylvia. Gerald and Brice were flying to Paris, where they were going to select the apartment in Paris where Brice and Eleanor would begin their married days and their university schedule. In Paris, they also planned to meet Brice's grandparents, whom they would accompany on the flight back to Newport. Philippe and Emmanuelle Fontaine were as elated as Gerald about the union of their grandson to Eleanor, a genteel heiress to the Marnham fortune.

Eleanor, Charlotte, and Sylvia were not traveling to Paris. They were busy with the wedding preparations. Charlotte and Eleanor were also preparing for the examinations that would allow Eleanor to move forward to her studies in the Sorbonne.

With Brice and Gerald busy in Paris and with Brice's parents, Damien and Adele, scheduled to arrive from Pittsburgh only a day or two before the wedding, Alan saw his opportunity. He wanted to initiate a private meeting with Eleanor. Before he could do that, though, he thought it essential that he meet with Charlotte, so that he could assure her that in his own way he still loved her. Of course, his love of her, platonic now rather than sensual, was not the kind of love she sought. Nevertheless, he needed to see her. Perhaps it was his guilt-stained conscience or a conventional sentimentality that compelled him to dine with her at their favorite Newport country club. Before they drove to the country club, he shared with her a conversation that he regarded as a farewell. There would be no other personal meetings between them. He intended to leave her to her own devices, as wily and self-serving as they usually were, for bringing new adventures into her life—the newness of which he would not be a part.

He entered her bedroom with casual assurance. He was wearing a lightweight beige summer suit, a yellow shirt, and a tie that blended beige and yellow geometric designs. Charlotte, looking especially glamorous in a floral evening dress, was seated before a vanity table applying gloss to her lips. She was surprised and pleased that he was paying a visit to her bedroom. Since his affair with Eleanor, he had rarely entered this room.

He began their conversation with forthright words and with the caring manner that, until his summer weeks with Eleanor, he had always brought to their marriage.

"I want to tell you some things that are better said here in the privacy of your bedroom, rather than at a banquet table in the country club."

Charlotte put aside her lip gloss and gave Alan her complete attention. She knew him well. He wanted to explain where he stood with her. He wanted to tell her why he was leaving their marriage. Her wise intuition and her keen-minded understanding of his troubled spirit helped her to maintain her equilibrium. Cautious and proficient, she needed to traverse the equivalent of a tightrope if she was to meet and to equal his hardened nature and to accept his world-weary appraisal of their intimate partnership.

"Go ahead," she said, prodding him forward. "Tell me what you've been planning to say for several weeks. Tell me all of it. I'm not brittle. I promise not to break apart."

"I'm not expecting you to break apart," he began. "I know you too well for that."

"What *do* you expect?"

"I expect you to be tough-willed and to hurry forward to a life without me. I expect you to understand that I have fallen in love with Eleanor and that I am planning to spend the rest of my days with her."

Charlotte carefully considered the heft and push of his remark. She answered him with the heft and push of her own words.

"In a few days, Eleanor will marry Brice. You won't

be part of her life anymore."

Maintaining a steady voice and a willful disposition, Alan responded with a remark that was both cynical and abrasive.

"Eleanor doesn't really love Brice. She has confused her schoolgirl infatuation with real love. I know her. I know that she is impressionable. I understand how easy it has been for Brice to play with her and to pretend that their relationship is the real thing. He's tricked her. He's enjoying the game. When he's no longer enjoying it, he will leave her. He will move on to some other debutante or chorus girl."

Charlotte became more insistent. Her perception of Brice's relationship with Eleanor and her willingness to accept the reality of their relationship was far different from his own viewpoint.

"Brice loves Eleanor. She loves him. She's finished with you. That's a hard truth to face, but—hard as it is— you must face it. You have to make a life without her."

Alan frowned. His voice stayed low, yet it suggested still the conflicted nature of his feelings and his inner turmoil.

"I can't live without Eleanor. My love for her isn't small or temporary or unimportant. She is my lifeline. Without her, there isn't any me anymore. There isn't any life worth living. There are only makeshift days ahead of me and bleak compromises. There is only a hollow man called Alan Aubray. The real Alan Aubray—the man I knew as a force of nature, the man that killed in order to stay alive, the man that pushed aside all obstacles and overcame all adversaries—will no longer exist. Without Eleanor, I'll be a walking dead man, a finished man who is trying to find his way out of a nightmare."

"What about us? What about the lives that we have shared through all the happy, carefree years and the war-torn ones, too?"

"I still love you. But I no longer need you. We cannot be happy together. There are too many war-horror memories that will always keep us from being truly happy. We need to break away from each other. You need to find the mate that will make your life new again. I've found Eleanor. She is my destiny. She is the woman who is meant to be with me for all the time that is left to me."

"What about Eleanor? Do you really understand how she feels? Can't you see that she has fallen in love with Brice? He is the man that destiny has planned for her."

"When she is with me, she doesn't think of Brice. She thinks only of me. I intend to talk with her. I'll make her see that marriage to Brice will be the worst thing she can do to herself. I'll convince her that I am the man that destiny has meant for her."

"You are fooling yourself, Alan. You are making yourself believe that Eleanor is the woman who will rescue you from your despair. But she can never rescue you. She isn't strong enough. She is nobody's rescuer. She is the one who needs to be rescued, and Brice Fontaine is the only man who can save her."

"I don't believe that. I believe in her and me together—in the here-and-now and for all eternity."

"What about you and me together? Don't you see anything good in those years we spent together?"

"I do. I still see all the years when we were happy—really happy together. I see us in Paris and in London, in Rome and New York and St. Moritz, and in all the other fabulous places that made our life together before the war both splendid and perfect."

"It can be that way again, if only you will believe in us. Right now, you are lost. Let me help you find your way back to your best self and to me. Let's make that journey together."

"I can't. I can't. I wouldn't even know how to begin."

"I'll help you find the way. Trust me, and we can make it happen."

She kissed him lightly on his lips. In this moment, she caressed more than kissed his lips. The touch of her lips upon his lips did stir him. The sensual part of his love for her was still alive. But his love for Eleanor had displaced it. He could not imagine that he would ever change his feelings. He could not imagine that he would try.

He did not want to make Charlotte more unhappy. He wanted her to find her way out of whatever darkness might overtake her when he was no longer with her.

He lightened the mood.

"Let's make tonight happen," he said. "Let's have a good time with our friends at the club."

They did have a good time. With their friends, they drank Champagne. They shared anecdotes about their life-quickening experiences before the war kayaking in Finland, hunting tigers in South Africa, scaling a mountain in Tibet, and flying in a hydrogen-filled balloon across San Francisco skies. Exhilarated, or seeming so on this evening five years after the war, they danced while a curvaceous blonde and a confident tenor—accompanied by a proficient orchestra—sang ballads about love that lasts forever. Never did Charlotte or Alan suggest to any of their friends that their marriage was in trouble. Always, their still-young faces beamed with happiness and with the pleasure of being so perfectly matched.

But Alan could not let go of his thoughts about Eleanor. He could not believe that Charlotte or any woman other than Eleanor could bring him the happiness that lasts forever.

The next afternoon, after he learned that in a few days Charlotte and Sylvia, as well as the housekeeper Mrs. Appleton, would be away on errands and appointments in nearby Middletown, he approached Eleanor about meeting him for the last time as a romantic partner with whom she had shared many pleasurable hours. She was standing alone by the blue-rimmed well in the rose garden while she read from a book of Elizabeth Barrett Browning's sonnets. He was aware that Eleanor planned to spend several days with friends in Nantucket. Now he urged her to return home earlier than she had planned. They two, alone together, could share several weekend hours that they might keep in their memory for all the time that they lived. At first, Eleanor was reluctant to break away from her friends only two days after her visit with them had begun. But, with smooth wiliness, he convinced her that their weekend meeting would provide a memorable closure to their love affair.

"It will be a happy meeting between us," he promised. "You can give me the gift of your love for one last time. Then I'll keep the memory of our last meeting forever. You owe me this one last time. You owe me because I love you so much. I'll love you until the end of time and even after that."

Immoral and self-centered and caught inside the fervor of Mrs. Browning's love poems, Eleanor quickly accepted his invitation. Though she genuinely loved Brice Fontaine, the man that she was going to marry at the end of the following week, she felt no compunction in sharing

Alan's bed for what he described as their farewell lovemaking. At least, she did not feel compunction right away. After all, Brice had shared his bed with many women. She imagined that, after she and Brice had been married for a year or two, he would share his bed with many young women he had not yet met. Betrayal of that sort was part of his nature. It was, she had to admit, part of her nature, too. After this special meeting with Alan, though, she was going to try to be faithful to Brice. She would try very hard.

But today was not the day that compunction was going to hold her back from her sensual inclinations.

"Let's do it," she told Alan after musing for a moment about their meeting for the last time as lovers. "Let's make an adventure."

On that sun-glittering afternoon when almost everyone was away from the house, they met on the beachfront of Gerald's property. Eleanor was wearing a form-fitting red bathing suit. Alan was wearing black trunks. From the moment that they sighted each other, exhilaration swept over them.

"I've missed you so much," Alan said as he caressed and then passionately kissed her. "Let's make this hour very special."

Quickly and completely, Eleanor was also caught inside the thrill of being with Alan. The thought that she had never stopped loving him stirred her reborn interest in him and her pleasure in being enfolded within his embrace. She returned his embrace and his kiss with an equal passion.

For their first hour together, they swam in the hastening blue-green waters of the ocean. They ran together on the white sands of the beach, carefree and agile and buoyant. They laughed together, and they sang together. They drank Champagne that Alan had carried to the beach inside an insulated wine bag. Eleanor recited some poems of which she was especially fond, including Elizabeth Barrett Browning's "If thou must love me, let it be for nought / Except for love's sake only"; Emily Dickinson's "I live with him, I see his face"; and Edna St. Vincent Millay's "If in the years to come you should recall."

They spoke of many things, including Alan's imaginative transformation of Gerald's estate and the success of Eleanor's studies with Charlotte and with him. Those challenges, Eleanor said, were completed achievements. She imagined that the future would bring them even more exciting challenges.

"The future is exciting," Alan said, "when it surprises us."

After their hour on the beach, Alan brought Eleanor to his bedroom. There, in an adjoining bathroom, they showered together and, with oversized comforting towels, dried each other's body. After that, Alan drew Eleanor into his bed and made vigorous love to her. Breathless because of the ecstasy to which he had brought her, Eleanor felt happier than she had ever felt. Alan felt happy, too. He was sated. He was satisfied. He intended never to lose this moment of supreme joy. Tenderly, he caressed Eleanor until she fell asleep in his arms. Then, after he reached for the snub-nosed revolver that lay waiting in the night table next to his bed, a .38 Smith and Wesson Special, he fired a bullet into Eleanor's heart. In nearly the same instant, he fired a bullet into his own heart. His body slumped over hers, as though he were still caressing her. The blood spilling out of their bodies met in a dark red stream.

Hours later, a policewoman who had been called to the scene with a group of policemen and a coroner, observed the bodies with unusual surprise. The naked bodies of Alan and Eleanor were clinging to each other, and their spilled blood had merged to make blood-dark stains upon the sheets. Though she made no remark to her peers, the well-read policewoman experienced an acute awareness that left her uneasy. The clinging bodies and the conjoined blood of the two lovers suggested an ancient sacrificial ritual.

EPILOGUE

When Gerald returned from Paris, his rigorous self-control served him as a well-trained sentry and as the stern arbiter of his conduct. During the police investigation of the killings, during the separate memorial services for Eleanor and Alan, and during a private conference with Brice, who had also returned from Paris and who shrouded himself inside a manly grief, Gerald refrained from emotional scenes and from any show of weakness. Instead, he took quick steps to console Charlotte especially and to persuade her that she had done no wrong. She was, he told her, in no way responsible for the tragedy that happened. Gray-faced and forlorn, Charlotte looked like a mere shadow of her former self. He intended to be her rescuer. Her here-on-Earth salvation would involve a move away from Newport. It would also include a new career and new friends.

He worked judiciously and made all the right moves. Within a few days, he arranged an entirely new scenario for Charlotte's life. Thus far, she had enriched her life with impressive and well-earned credentials. In Paris, she had studied at the Sorbonne. At Ardennes, Verdun, the Somme, the Marne, and Soissons during the recent war, she had proved her courage as a nurse at the rim of savage fields of battle. At The Newbury School in Manhattan, one of the best private schools in the United States, she had served as a meticulous teacher. Four months ago, she rescued Eleanor from suicidal intentions. The tragedy that overtook Eleanor two weeks ago was none of Charlotte's doing. She must believe that. Only then could she go forward.

Charlotte needed to create a new path for herself. He, Gerald Marnham—the CEO of the estimable Marnham Steel Corporation—was going to guide her on to that path. He was offering her a position as a public relations officer within his corporation. There would be several immersive weeks of training and several exciting weeks of meeting the many people who were going to become essential to her everyday happiness. Multi-lingual and articulate, she was going to make a favorable impression upon corporate leaders across the globe. She would, of course, make her new home in Pittsburgh. But business travel to many countries was in her future. With his cherished Sylvia, he was also going to guide her into the company of the eligible men who would help her to regain her happiness—or at least an acceptable semblance of happiness.

Emotionally benumbed, Charlotte listened to his plan. At first, she said nothing, although she was grateful that he was offering her this rescuing plan. Then, because she was beginning to know the horror and anguish of

Alan's abandonment of her by means of his death, she suddenly felt the need of being rescued, if only that were possible. In the next instant, she acceded to Gerald's plan.

"I'll do whatever you say," she told him. "I need to be reborn. I need to become somebody else."

"Of course, you do, my dear," Sylvia said, her voice filled with pity and affection. "Of course, you do."

"You will make a new life for yourself," Gerald encouraged her. "You may even learn how to be happy again."

Hearing his words, Charlotte offered him a polite smile. She wanted him to believe that the days and months and years ahead of her would validate his predictions. But she did not believe that anyone or anything could rescue her. Alan had died. Eleanor had died. Nothing could bring them back. Death had claimed them quickly. The years of anguish to which her destiny condemned her would not release their hold upon her. Her death would last many years—a death-in-life that meted out painful regrets, anguished memories, and bitter awareness. For her, there might well be the surface joys of corporate success. There would surely be glamorous settings for her achievements, an impressive portfolio of stocks, bonds, and real estate holdings, and a gallery of equally wealthy friends. There might also be her intimate couplings with the many men and a few more husbands who shared with her weeks and months and even a few years of plausible contentment and who took from her body the temporary pleasure she offered them and afterwards—after the weeks and months and years of makeshift contentment and after the excited consummations and post-coital ease—went their separate ways.

"You *will* make a new life," Sylvia promised her, "and you *will* be happy, too."

Charlotte smiled again, as though she were quietly consenting to Sylvia's and Gerald's wish for her.

Now, Sylvia said something more.

"The important thing is to hurry past this horrible tragedy that has happened."

"It *is* horrible," Gerald agreed, "and it defies reason. I still can't quite fathom it. I don't understand how Alan could kill a girl that he loved so much."

"Eleanor was also the girl that he could no longer call his own," Sylvia explained, "at least not while she lived. She was the girl who had fallen in love with another man."

"It defies reason, I say."

"It was his fate," Sylvia said. "It was the destiny he chose for himself."

Charlotte listened carefully as she consented to Sylvia's words.

"Killing himself and the young woman he loved was Alan's destiny. There were persons and circumstances in his environment that influenced that destiny. Alan did not need to choose that destiny. He could have chosen a destiny without the violence and without the deaths. Alan understood that. He chose the destiny that would rescue him from despair and chose, too, the astonishment of its ending. He saw that ending as the only one he could choose. He couldn't live with the young woman that he loved, and he couldn't live without her. In that moment of dying with her, they belonged to each other eternally. In that final moment, right after they made love, he experienced a lasting happiness. For that moment, he paid the price."

"The price?" Gerald asked.

"Yes," Sylvia answered him. "For Alan, *death* was the price of happiness."

AN ALTERNATE NARRATIVE FOR THE READER
WHO BELIEVES IN HAPPIER ENDINGS

With Brice and Gerald busy in Paris and with Brice's parents, Damien and Adele, scheduled to arrive from Pittsburgh only a day or two before the wedding, Alan saw his opportunity. He wanted to initiate a private meeting with Eleanor. Before he could do that, though, he thought it essential that he meet with Charlotte, so that he could assure her that in his own way he still loved her. Of course, his love of her, platonic now rather than sensual, was not the kind of love she sought. Nevertheless, he needed to see her. Perhaps it was his guilt-stained conscience or a conventional sentimentality that compelled him to dine with her at their favorite Newport country club. Before they drove to the country club, he shared with her a conversation that he regarded as a farewell. There would be no other personal meetings between them. He intended to leave her to her own devices, as wily and self-serving as they usually were, for bringing new adventures into her life—the newness of which he would not be a part.

He entered her bedroom with casual assurance. He was wearing a lightweight beige summer suit, a yellow shirt, and a tie that blended beige and yellow geometric designs. Charlotte, looking especially glamorous in a floral evening dress, was seated before a vanity table applying gloss to her lips. She was surprised and pleased that he was paying a visit to her bedroom. Since his affair with Eleanor, he had rarely entered this room.

He began their conversation with forthright words and with the caring manner that, until his summer weeks with Eleanor, he had always brought to their marriage.

"I want to tell you some things that are better said here in the privacy of your bedroom, rather than at a banquet table in the country club."

Charlotte put aside her lip gloss and gave Alan her complete attention. She knew him well. He wanted to explain where he stood with her. He wanted to tell her why he was leaving their marriage. Her wise intuition and her keen-minded understanding of his troubled spirit helped her to maintain her equilibrium. Cautious and proficient, she needed to traverse the equivalent of a tightrope if she was to meet and to equal his hardened nature and to accept his world-weary appraisal of their intimate partnership.

"Go ahead," she said, prodding him forward. "Tell me what you've been planning to say for several weeks. Tell me all of it. I'm not brittle. I promise not to break apart."

"I'm not expecting you to break apart," he began. "I know you too well for that."

"What do you expect?"

"I expect you to be tough-willed and to hurry forward to a life without me. I expect you to understand that I have fallen in love with Eleanor and that I am planning to spend the rest of my days with her."

Charlotte carefully considered the heft and push of his remark. She answered him with the heft and push of her own words.

"In a few days, Eleanor will marry Brice. You won't be part of her life anymore."

Maintaining a steady voice and a willful disposition, Alan responded with a remark that was both cynical and abrasive.

"Eleanor doesn't really love Brice. She has confused her schoolgirl infatuation with real love. I know her. I know that she is impressionable. I understand how easy it has been for Brice to play with her and to pretend that their relationship is the real thing. He's tricked her. He's enjoying the game. When he's no longer enjoying it, he will leave her. He will move on to some other debutante or chorus girl."

Charlotte became more insistent. Her perception of Brice's relationship with Eleanor and her willingness to accept the reality of their relationship was far different from his own viewpoint.

"Brice loves Eleanor. She loves him. She's finished with you. That's a hard truth to face, but—hard as it is— you must face it. You have to make a life without her."

Alan frowned. His voice stayed low, yet it suggested still the conflicted nature of his feelings and his inner turmoil.

"I can't live without Eleanor. My love for her isn't small or temporary or unimportant. She is my lifeline. Without her, there isn't any me anymore. There isn't any life worth living. There are only makeshift days ahead of me and bleak compromises. There is only a hollow man called Alan Aubray. The real Alan Aubray—the man I knew as a force of nature, the man that killed in order to stay alive, the man that pushed aside all obstacles and overcame all adversaries—will no longer exist. Without Eleanor, I'll be a walking dead man, a finished man who is trying to find his way out of a nightmare."

"What about us? What about the lives that we have shared through all the happy, carefree years and the war-torn ones, too?"

"I still love you. But I no longer need you. We cannot be happy together. There are too many war-horror memories that will always keep us from being truly happy. We need to break away from each other. You need to find the mate that will make your life new again. I've found Eleanor. She is my destiny. She is the woman who is meant to be with me for all the time that is left to me."

"What about Eleanor? Do you really understand how she feels? Can't you see that she has fallen in love with Brice? He is the man that destiny has planned for her."

"When she is with me, she doesn't think of Brice. She thinks only of me. I intend to talk with her. I'll make her see that marriage to Brice will be the worst thing she can do to herself. I'll convince her that I am the man that destiny has meant for her."

"You are fooling yourself, Alan. You are making yourself believe that Eleanor is the woman who will rescue you from your despair. But she can never rescue you. She isn't strong enough. She is nobody's rescuer. She is the one who needs to be rescued, and Brice Fontaine is the only man who can save her."

"I don't believe that. I believe in her and me together—in the here-and-now and for all eternity."

"What about you and me together? Don't you see anything good in those years we spent together?"

"I do. I still see all the years when we were happy—really happy together. I see us in Paris and in London, in Rome and New York and St. Moritz, and in all the other fabulous places that made our life together before the war both splendid and perfect."

"It can be that way again, if only you will believe in us. Right now, you are lost. Let me help you find your way back to your best self and to me. Let's make that journey together."

"I can't. I can't. I wouldn't even know how to begin."

"I'll help you find the way. Trust me, and we can make it happen."

She kissed him lightly on his lips. In this moment, she caressed more than kissed his lips. The touch of her lips upon his lips did stir him. The sensual part of his love for her was still alive. But his love for Eleanor had displaced it. He could not imagine that he would ever change his feelings. He could not imagine that he would try.

He did not want to make Charlotte more unhappy. He wanted her to find her way out of whatever darkness might overtake her when he was no longer with her.

He lightened the mood.

"Let's make tonight happen," he said. "Let's have a good time with our friends at the club."

They did have a good time. With their friends, they drank Champagne. They shared anecdotes about their life-quickening experiences before the war kayaking in Finland, hunting tigers in South Africa, scaling a mountain in Tibet, and flying in a hydrogen-filled balloon across San Francisco skies. Exhilarated, or seeming so on this evening five years after the war, they danced while a curvaceous blonde and a confident tenor—accompanied by a proficient orchestra— sang ballads about love that lasts forever. Never did

Charlotte or Alan suggest to any of their friends that their marriage was in trouble. Always, their still-young faces beamed with happiness and with the pleasure of being so perfectly matched.

But Alan could not let go of his thoughts about Eleanor. He could not believe that Charlotte or any woman other than Eleanor could bring him the happiness that lasts forever.

The next afternoon, after he learned that in a few days Charlotte and Sylvia, as well as the housekeeper Mrs. Appleton, would be away on errands and appointments in nearby Middletown, he approached Eleanor about meeting him for the last time as a romantic partner with whom she had shared many pleasurable hours. She was standing alone by the blue-rimmed well in the rose garden while she read from a book of Elizabeth Barrett Browning's sonnets. He was aware that Eleanor planned to spend several days with friends in Nantucket. Now he urged her to return home earlier than she had planned. They two, alone together, could share several weekend hours that they might keep in their memory for all the time that they lived. At first, Eleanor was reluctant to break away from her friends only two days after her visit with them had begun. But, with smooth wiliness, he convinced her that their weekend meeting would provide a memorable closure to their love affair.

"It will be a happy meeting between us," he promised. "You can give me the gift of your love for one last time. Then I'll keep the memory of our last meeting forever. You owe me this one last time. You owe me because I love you so much. I'll love you until the end of time and even after that."

Amoral and self-centered and caught inside the fervor of Mrs. Browning's love poems, Eleanor quickly accepted his invitation. Though she genuinely loved Brice Fontaine, the man that she was going to marry at the end of the following week, she felt no compunction in sharing Alan's bed for what he described as their farewell lovemaking. At least, she did not feel compunction right away. After all, Brice had shared his bed with many women. She imagined that, after she and Brice had been married for a year or two, he would share his bed with many young women he had not yet met. Betrayal of that sort was part of his nature. It was, she had to admit, part of her nature, too. After this special meeting with Alan, though, she was going to try to be faithful to Brice. She would try very hard.

But today was not the day that compunction was going to hold her back from her sensual inclinations.

"Let's do it," she told Alan after musing for a moment about their meeting for the last time as lovers. "Let's make an adventure."

On that sun-glittering afternoon when almost everyone was away from the house, they met on the beachfront of Gerald's property. Eleanor was wearing a form-fitting red bathing suit. Alan was wearing black trunks. From the moment that they sighted each other, exhilaration swept over them.

"I've missed you so much," Alan said as he caressed and then passionately kissed her. "Let's make this hour very special."

Quickly and completely, Eleanor was also caught inside the thrill of being with Alan. The thought that she had never stopped loving him stirred her reborn interest in him and her pleasure in being enfolded within his embrace. She returned his embrace and his kiss with an equal passion.

For their first hour together, they swam in the hastening blue-green waters of the ocean. They ran together on the white sands of the beach, carefree and agile and buoyant. They laughed together, and they sang together. They drank Champagne that Alan had carried to the beach inside an insulated wine bag. Eleanor recited some poems of which she was especially fond, including Elizabeth Barrett Browning's "If thou must love me, let it be for nought / Except for love's sake only"; Emily Dickinson's "I live with him, I see his face"; and Edna St. Vincent Millay's "If in the years to come you should recall."

They spoke of many things, including Alan's imaginative transformation of Gerald's estate and the success of Eleanor's studies with Charlotte and with him. Those challenges, Eleanor said, were completed achievements. She imagined that the future would bring them even more exciting challenges.

"The future is exciting," Alan said, "when it surprises us."

After their hour on the beach, Alan brought Eleanor to his bedroom. There, in an adjoining bathroom, they showered together and, with oversized comforting towels, dried each other's body. After that, Alan drew Eleanor into his bed and made vigorous love to her. Breathless because of the ecstasy to which he had brought her, Eleanor felt happier than she had ever felt. Alan felt happy, too. He was sated. He was satisfied. He intended never to lose this moment of supreme joy. Tenderly, he caressed Eleanor until she fell asleep in his arms.

Then, because he had carefully planned this nightmarish scenario, he reached for the snub-nosed revolver that lay waiting in the night table next to his bed, a .38 Smith and Wesson Special. He placed all four fingers of his hand under the trigger guard and pressed his index finger hard underneath it. He had only to press the trigger straight to the rear, increase the pressure, and fire the pistol. He was going to fire a bullet into Eleanor's heart. In nearly the same instant, he would fire a bullet into his own heart. His body would slump over hers, as though he were still caressing her. The blood spilling out of their bodies would meet in a dark red stream.

But he did not fire the pistol.

Something or someone stopped him from firing. Perhaps, it was a memory held inside the shadows of his conscience. Yes, it was that—the memory of something—the recent war—and of someone—the rugged face and brawny physique of a fellow lieutenant, vivid and brutalized inside the recollection of a muddied battlefield strewn with the corpses of young soldiers, the booming sounds of the howitzer cannons hurling their deadly projectiles, the wailing of high, far-traveling shrapnel shells, the rapid rattle of stuttering rifles and, closer than that, the sound and sight of dark blood gargling and spilling from a pale recruit's lungs corrupted by poison gas.

That memory with its ghostly images stopped him.

The rugged, battle-scarred face of that lieutenant rose before him, vivid and heroic. It was he, this quick-thinking lieutenant, who had sacrificed himself when he threw his big-boned body upon a grenade so that he could save four war-hardened men including *him*, Alan Aubray, whom the war had made more cynical and more bitter than his earlier, comfortable life had taught him to be. It was the memory of that lieutenant on a corpse-strewn battlefield bellowing a lifesaving warning just before he threw himself upon an exploding grenade—it was that memory that stopped him from pressing the trigger that would fire a bullet into Eleanor's heart and afterward into his own heart.

For just this instant, he loved Eleanor more than he loved himself.

He was not going to kill her. He had already killed too many human beings on battlefields that still haunted him. The young, boyish bodies of his enemy-victims haunted him most of all. He had trained himself as much as he could to forget the killings. Yet his many acts of killing still clung to him. Perhaps, they would always invade his dreams. They would always influence the unanticipated hours of his melancholy. He was almost used to losing things. The world was, after all, a skillful thief. The war had stolen the quiet soulfulness he had often experienced through the comforting days of his boyhood. The war and its aftermath had robbed him of his belief that his marriage to Charlotte would bring the two of them a forever-after happiness. It wasn't the war alone, of course, or the savagery in the world that had robbed him of authentic happiness. They *were* thieves. They *had* robbed him of his best hopes and aspirations. They *had* tarnished the purity of his marriage to Charlotte.

But he was his own thief. He had robbed himself of hope in his future. He had refused the gift of love when

Charlotte had so patiently offered that gift to him. Now he was stealing Eleanor from Brice, who for the first time—without duplicity or selfishness—was really learning to love a woman. Not only was he stealing Eleanor from Brice. He was stealing Brice from Eleanor and all their happy years together. He was also stealing Eleanor's life—depriving her of the happiness that was going to play a large part in her future and, yes, stealing from her the adventures that would help her to grow self-determining and strong through good times and troubled times, as well.

No, he did not fire the bullet into Eleanor's heart or into his own.

He returned the pistol to its place inside the drawer of the bedside table. He noticed the stillness in the room and the afternoon sun glowing through the panoramic window and granting this bedroom a nearly enchanted radiance. Eleanor looked enchanted, her blonde beauty and her serene expression accepting the solace of temporary sleep, with its promise of new-born awakening and the reality of lovely perfect days and, possibly, a few too-venturous, imperfect ones.

He leaned toward Eleanor and kissed her lightly upon her forehead. So light was his kiss that she did not stir awake. Her unawareness of him was, he felt, an appropriate finish to their relationship.

He left the room and made his way to Gerald's

study, where he would busy himself with architectural plans for future engineering assignments and architectural landscaping designs. Later, he would greet Charlotte with a new fervor. He would learn, once again, how to be faithful to his patient wife.

Maybe this time the world was not stealing from him. Maybe, because of his memories of the rough-hewn lieutenant who had saved him and the encouragement of strong-willed Charlotte and the promises of a life-enhancing future, he could move forward with his best capacities and his well-worn tenacity. He was going to keep in mind that nothing comes free. For him, the price of happiness was the death of his selfish ways. That price demanded *self*-sacrifice. He would bear up. He would learn how to be happy in spite of his war memories and in spite of losing the sometimes-love of an impressionable young woman named Eleanor. He would learn how to love Charlotte in the fervent way that he had first loved her, when they were very young and when the world had not stolen their innocent beliefs and their untarnished dreams.